End of Cycles

End of Cycles

BOOK 3 OF THE MOON CYCLE TRILOGY

J.R. Shepherd

Contents

Prologue

1	Chapter One	5
2	Chapter Two	19
3	Chapter Three	34
4	Chapter Four	49
5	Chapter Five	68
6	Chapter Six	91
7	Chapter Seven	109
8	Chapter Eight	129
9	Chapter Nine	147
10	Chapter Ten	162
11	Chapter Eleven	176
12	Chapter Twelve	192
13	Chapter Thirteen	206

vi - Contents

Epilogue

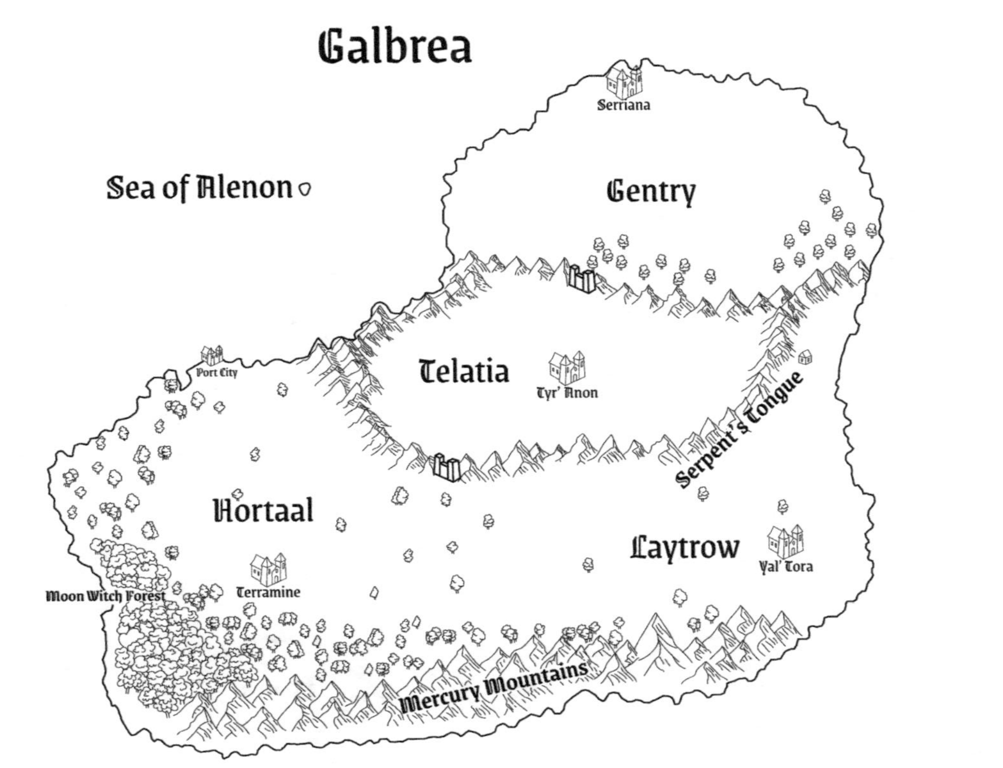

Galbrea
Sea of Alenon
Gentry
Serriana
Telatia
Tyr' Anon
Port City
Hortaal
Serpent's Tongue
Laytrow
Val' Tora
Moon Witch Forest
Terramine
Mercury Mountains

Prologue

Rielle stood in the center of the town square, sword drawn, her eyes crazed. Her skin was pale in the faint moonlight, and her face was gaunt with hunger. The villagers stood around her, watching in fear, as she lashed out at any who moved.

Several guards stood between her and the people, trying to keep her at bay with their spears. Vesth clenched his hands and reached for his own sword. A dark hand grasped his wrist.

"You cannot stop her." Vesth growled and tried to shake off the hand.

"Let go of me Keliter, I have to try." The hand did not loosen it's grasp.

"You don't have the strength to beat her. You cannot open enough gates to match her yet." Vesth glanced back at the Telatian in mild surprise.

"What would you know." Keliter met his gaze coldly.

"I know that you would need to open at least your fourth gate to match the speed of the Cloak of the Wind. As of now you can only control your strength up to the third. I also know that you are likely the only one who can get to the last remaining scraps of her sanity. But in order for you to speak to her, she would have to be subdued." Vesth once again pulled at the hand that held him.

"Then let me do this."

"No." Keliter commanded, pulling him back into the alley. Then the Telatian stepped forward, drawing the long knife from his belt, the rearing dragon on the blade brightly reflecting the moon and stars.

"Let me."

1

∽

Chapter One

"Using this formation a small group can hold a much larger force at bay." Segine pointed out the position of each soldier on the battlefield map laid out on the table.

"Creating the wedge will force a charging enemy force to divide and weaken their front line. However, this tactic should not be used while strategic retreat is still an option, since the group becomes surrounded and must either win the battle or die trying." The men around him nodded their understanding.

"Sergeant Memoria." A man wearing a messenger sash trotted into the training yard and approached Segine.

"What is it?" The man pressed his fist against his chest in salute.

"Brother Aegis wishes to speak with you and your companion once you are done for the day." Segine nodded and waved to dismiss the messenger. The man nodded and quickly carried on with his other tasks. Segine turned back to the men around him.

"Be sure to teach your men these formations and how to use them. Holding mock battles in different scenarios would likely be a good way to begin. I want them proficient so that if I give the order they can move without hesitation. Hesitation on the battlefield will end in death." The men around him nodded their understanding. Segine nodded in return and then waved his hand.

"Good, you are dismissed." The men left the training field and each went their separate ways. Segine sighed and cleared the figures from the table, glancing across the field as he did.

Nysisset stood at the other end, sword in hand, instructing a dozen or so men in its use. She drilled them over and over again, forcing them to repeat each set of movements until she was satisfied that they understood.

Segine finished as the sun was setting and watched as Nysisset sent the battered and exhausted men away. She slammed her sword into it's scabbard and stomped towards Segine.

"I cannot believe that men who claim to be warriors can be so incompetent with a blade in their hands." She complained once he was within earshot.

"I had Hoped when the High King told us we would be training with the army of the Brotherhood that there would be at least a few proficient warriors. But no, of course not. They are all as useless as children. They have no discipline, they are far from physically powerful, and they probably wouldn't know which way to point their swords if they were in actual combat." Nysisset dropped herself into a seat near the table and frowned. Segine tied off the bag that held the figures of the soldiers and set it beneath the table.

"At least you have gotten it through their heads that you are a skilled fighter, even though you are a woman." Nysisset scoffed.

"Narrow-minded dullards, the lot of them." Segine shrugged and picked his sword up from its place beside the table and tied it to his side.

"Perhaps we should have a Dragon's Blade crafted for you, I am sure Brother Aegis could convince the High King to grant you one." Nysisset frowned again.

"I have no need for such trinkets. I see no point in such a frivolous decoration." Segine finished tying his sword on.

"But if you had one, even the men would not be able to deny your skill, and they would likely take your instruction more seriously." Nysisset sighed grumpily.

"What a hassle." Segine shrugged.

"It probably wouldn't be difficult to convince the High King. As far as I have seen you are more skilled with a blade than I, and likely almost as good as Vesth." Nysisset glared at Segine from the corner of her eye. A few weeks ago, he might have hurriedly apologized for being rude, but he had since learned that it just made things worse.

"I mean you no disrespect, But I have seen Vesth's skill first hand, and as good as you are I still think Vesth would win a duel between the two of you." Nysisset stuck her nose in the air.

"Well that just shows how much you know." She stood up and straightened her tunic. "Well, I am hungry. I am going to go find something to eat." Segine nodded and stood aside for her.

"Oh, once you are done with that, Brother Aegis sent word that he wishes to meet with both of us." Nysisset let out an aggravated sigh.

"What does the Old Coot want now?" Segine just shrugged.

"I was not informed why, only that he wished to speak with us once the day was through." Nysisset grumbled.

"Fine. I will find you after I eat." She slipped away into the fading evening light and Segine turned to go in search of his room and a wash basin. Once he had washed and found a fresh shirt, he stepped outside and looked up at the starlit sky. He looked over the constellations, remembering his father teaching him each of their names and the time of year they appeared in the sky.

"You look like an idiot staring straight up like that." Segine looked back down and his eyes followed the sound of the voice. Nysisset stood in the shadows of a building, chewing on a heel of bread.

"You really shouldn't hang your mouth open when you look at the sky, you look like a fish out of water." Segine frowned. Nysisset half smiled, obviously enjoying teasing him.

"Well let's go, Knight. I don't want to be waiting around all night to see the Old Coot." Segine sighed and followed quietly. They walked around the small buildings and narrow streets, heading towards the center of the makeshift town where the large command building was located. When they entered, they were led down a few halls to a large room with heavy oaken doors and told to wait until they were summoned. Nysisset grumbled, her eyes fading between light and dark shades of violet. Segine carefully reached out and pulled her hand away from the amulet that hung around her neck. She didn't seem to notice.

It was not very long before the doors opened and several men left the room and went their seperate ways.

"Come in Sir Segine, and please close the doors behind you if you would." A tall man with gray hair and a well trimmed beard waved to them from his place behind a large desk. Segine nodded and followed Nysisset inside, pulling the doors shut behind them.

"What did you wish to discuss with us Brother Aegis?" Segine asked politely.

"Yes," Nysisset scowled. "Please enlighten us." Brother Aegis nodded. He was a fairly serious man, and nothing seemed to bother his cool exterior.

"There were a few things, actually. First, I received a package for the two of you. An old gentleman delivered it this morning when he traveled through town with his cart. He said to tell you that it was from the temple, though he did not specify which temple it was from." Nysisset grumbled.

"Did he have a beard, gray hair, claim to be a traveling salesman, and have a mischievous glint in his eyes?" Brother Aegis nodded.

"He did." Nysisset groaned. Segine frowned at her and then nodded to Brother Aegis.

"We know where it came from." Brother Aegis nodded and pulled a long slender package from beside the desk and held it out to them. Segine accepted it and noticed a small envelope tied to the top. Nysisset took the envelope and slid a note out, quickly reading over it. Grumbling she held it out to Segine and took the package from him. Segine read it over once and then, with a nod from Brother Aegis, read it aloud.

"To Segine and Nysisset, I bring this package to you at the request of my elder siblings. Inside you will find two items for Nysisset, forged by Marina and enchanted by Solidus. In time Marina also plans to forge a new set of armor for both of you, which you will receive in due time. One of the two items is to prepare Nysisset for the coming Dark Moon Cycle. The other should be self explanatory. Also included are two letters penned by Solidus. One for you, and one for the man called Brother Aegis. Be sure he gets it please and thank you. Signed, Delgorin." Nysisset broke the string that tied the package shut and pulled off the outer cover to reveal a polished wooden box.

She pulled off the lid, handing it to Segine and frowning at the contents. Segine took the lid, then the two letters that Nysisset held out, uncomfortably close to his face. Segine took the first letter and handed it to Brother Aegis and opened the other. With another nod from Brother Aegis, Segine read it aloud.

"Greetings to you Segine and Nysisset. Within this box you will find a small silver cage and a Dragon Blade." Segine paused and looked at Nysisset. She tilted the box so he could see inside. At the bottom sat two white velvet bags, one the length of the box, the other only a few inches long.

"Strange that Master Solidus would send us a Dragon Blade on the same day we considered having one made for you." Nysisset sniffed spitefully.

"Not surprising at all. Master Solidus probably thought about it when he decided to send us here in the first place." Segine shrugged and looked to Brother Aegis.

"Am I to assume that the sword was created by Forge

Mistress Marina? Blacksmith for the Temple of Fire and Earth?" Segine nodded.

"Yes sir. I hadn't realized she was so well known." Brother Aegis nodded.

"She is the one from whom the Four Countries request the Dragon's Blades. Her smithing skills are unmatched, and no one else remembers how the Dragon's Blades are forged save her." Segine felt his eyebrows rise, though he didn't feel like he should be all that surprised.

"Continue Sir Segine." Segine nodded and continued reading.

"The silver cage opens from one side and should be placed around the amulet. Once closed, it will not open again, and it will prevent the dark power in the stone from taking control during the Dark Moon Cycle or in places of darkness or strong taint. The power will still be accessible to Nysisset so tell her that she may stop frowning now." Segine glanced up out of the corner of his eye to see that Nysisset was indeed frowning deeply at the letter. Segine quickly continued.

"Also, once you receive this, things will be set in motion. The army of the Brotherhood should move and make their main camp at the Great Southwestern Gate and wait until the time is right. They will be joined there by armies from Hortaal and Laytrow. The two of you will need to take your leave of them once they make camp and travel east along the Serpent Tongue mountains until you reach the path to the Temple of Fire and Earth. Make your camp in front of Tiamat's cave and wait there until told otherwise. It will not be too long. Other details will be in the letter I have written to Brother Aegis. Signed, Pravin Solidus." Segine looked up from the letter. Brother Aegis was obviously not very pleased, but thought silently to himself for several minutes before speaking.

"How well do you know this Solidus?" The older man watched Segine fidget uncomfortably.

"It is a difficult question to answer. I myself have only known Master Solidus for a short while. I have simply followed the orders he has given, and though there have been times when I did not understand his actions, he has yet to lead us astray." Brother Aegis nodded and looked to Nysisset.

"And you? I assume you know more than Sir Segine." Nysisset huffed.

"What makes you think that Old Coot?" Brother Aegis opened a drawer in his desk and reached inside.

"It should come as no surprise to you that I have studied many things in my lifetime. I have read books stored in the Great library in Serriana, and a few from Terramine that predate the Purge. I recognize the Brand of Khornal, Deity of Darkness, that you try to hide on your neck." Nysisset's eyes narrowed.

"What of my Brand? Such a thing has not been seen since long before the purge. How would you know of it?" Brother Aegis pulled a small, and obviously very old, book from his desk and placed it in front of him.

"I received this book some few weeks ago from one of my oldest students. It was accompanied by a letter stating it was from one, Pravin Solidus, and should be thoroughly studied. I went through the effort of looking into his background, but the only Solidus I could find was the Teacher of High King Hortaal." Nysisset eyed the book carefully.

"He is the same." Brother Aegis studied her face.

"How is that possible?" Nyssiset's eyes shifted and finally met with Brother Aegis.

"You are meddling in affairs not meant for mortals. You should stop digging before you find something that should not be found." Segine did not like how serious Nysisset's voice had become. Brother Aegis met her gaze calmly.

"I do not intend to take orders from a man who I can, in no way, prove to be just. If you cannot give me the information I need to make that decision then I will be forced to treat him as a threat." Nysisset's eyes grew dark and the air in the room became heavy. Whispers filled the room when Nysisset spoke.

"Grandmaster Silver Mage, Pravin Solidus was born in the Age of Creation in the Kingdom of Alenon. He was raised in the High Temple and found to have the potential for becoming a Balance Mage. When the People of Alenon attacked the other kingdoms in an effort to stamp out evil and bring all into their righteous control, The Deity of Good destroyed Alenon and sank it into the sea. Only four survived, the closest servants of the Deity of Good herself. The eldest was Pravin Solidus.

They were given tasks to perform and were sent out into the world. Master Solidus is tasked with protecting the Balance of the world. He directs those who can change the Balance so that they may keep this world from destruction. His power is unfathomable, his intellect unmatched, and he is far beyond your mortal power to oppose.

If his intention was to destroy you, he would have. And you would not be able to stand in his way. I suggest you follow his orders or he will find someone else who will and he will leave you by the wayside to face the demons and their hosts on your own." Nysisset turned to leave and paused at the door.

"Segine, finish your business here, we must speak." With this said, she opened the door and left. Segine was slightly stunned, and was unable to move until Brother Aegis spoke again.

"Does she speak the truth?" Segine took a deep breath and straightened, standing to fill his large frame.

"I cannot speak for everything she said, but I have been to the High Temple in Alenon and met the four mages who called Alenon their home. I have stood in the Presence of Lord Tiamat and Lord Leviathan. I have met the four rulers of the Kingdoms and I have even laid my eyes upon Necrotic Dracolich Khornal. All of them hold Master Solidus in the highest respect. If a man of such great influence and power asks me to act, I will gladly lay my life down on his behalf." As he spoke, Segine's eyes and expression hardened like stone. Brother Aegis looked back down at the unopened letter on his desk.

"And you are positive he fights to protect the world?" Segine nodded.

"I have also been to Tyr' Anon and stood before High Priest Borsa. The Taint he brings into this world is most foul and he will stop at nothing to destroy everything that stands in his path to power. Master Solidus knows how to fight him, and I fear his power will likely be the only thing that saves us in the end." Segine turned to the door and paused as his hand began to pull it open.

"I trust Master Solidus... And So does Vesth." Brother Aegis looked back to Segine. "You may not trust Master Solidus but, don't you trust your student?" Without waiting for a reply Segine left, pulling the door closed behind him. He followed the halls and stepped out into the night air.

Nysisset stood waiting, an elegant longsword in her hand.

She pulled the blade from it's scabbard and inspected the rearing dragon at it's base.

"Are you finished?" She asked, not looking at him but instead returning the sword to it's scabbard and sliding it back into the velvet bag it had come in. Segine nodded.

"Good." Nysisset looked up at the sky and then down at Segine. "The Dark Moon Cycle is close, if you do not want a repeat of what happened last time I suggest you come with me and help me to seal my amulet." Segine nodded.

"What has changed your demeanor?" He asked quietly. Nysisset looked back into the sky.

"I can hear the Whispers of great Master Khornal. Something is changing in the winds. This fight is becoming something beyond us. The world heaves and creaks, and the elements shift, trying to maintain balance."

"What is it?" Segine asked quietly. Nysisset looked back at Segine and, for an instant, he saw worry on her face.

"It is the upheaval caused by the coming of a Prediction. It will not be long now before it reaches a conclusion, and the fate of the world will be decided." Nysisset reached up and held out the small, white velvet bag. "We must be ready." Segine nodded, holding out his hand and accepting the bag. Nysisset placed it carefully in his palm, pausing for a moment as their hands met, and then turned away.

"Lets go, we have things to do, and I need sleep before we move out tomorrow." Segine followed silently, contemplating what was expected of them. A few moments passed and then he heard a quiet melody. He raised his head and the weight on his heart lifted slightly as Nysisset softly sang.

* * *

Vesth still had reservations about his new traveling companion, even though Keliter kept a respectful distance as he busied himself cleaning up their camp. Vesth watched the man as he worked, his sand colored cloak waving behind him as he moved.

It was obvious to Vesth that Keliter was a skilled fighter, as his movements were always balanced and smooth, and his right hand never strayed too far from the long knife at his side.

"You are sure this is the right place?" Keliter nodded as he rolled his bedding and tied it to his pack.

"I am positive. Your companion will pass through the nearby town tonight. It is likely to cause quite a stir." Vesth eyed the man, he still felt that he recognized the man from somewhere.

"How do you know these things?" Keliter spared him a glance.

"Would you believe that I just know?" Vesth waited without a response. Keliter shrugged and went back to his pack.

"Let us say I can sense things. How they affect each other, their push and pull you might say." Vesth considered this.

"So you can sense the balance then?" Keliter nodded.

"Simply put, yes. Though I am obviously not like Master Solidus. I cannot see the threads of the balance, but I can feel where the balance is weighted. Your friend carries a great deal of weight in the balance, so she is easy to follow." Vesth thought for a few moments and then nodded.

"I can accept that explanation for now." Keliter finished tying his pack and slipped it onto his back.

"Shall we move out then Captain?" Vesth mounted his horse with a nod, and they moved out of the clearing they had spent the night in and back out onto the road. They traveled in silence, Keliter staying several paces behind Vesth as they went.

When they entered the town Vesth noticed that everything seemed far too quiet. A few people and guards roamed the streets, but everything was still and somber. No one spoke, no one motioned to anyone else, no one even seemed to acknowledge that anyone else existed.

Vesth frowned, and turned towards what he took as the inn. He tied his horse at a watering trough and made his way inside.

The dining room was empty and the innkeeper stood behind his counter, mindlessly wiping a mug with a thin rag.

"Do you have rooms available for the night?" The innkeeper stared at him blankly.

"You got gold?" Vesth frowned at the man, reaching into a pouch at his side and pulling out a small bag, making sure the coins inside jingled as he did. A faint spark glinted in the inkeeper's eye.

"Aye, we have a room available." Vesth was already not liking the way the man was eyeing him.

"Then I need the room for two men and a hot meal for both as well." He tossed the bag of gold onto the counter and it quickly disappeared under the man's apron.

"Of course sir, I will stoke the cooking fire immediately." The innkeeper said with a grin, showing his rotting teeth. Vesth nodded, removing his cloak and making sure the innkeeper saw the sword at his side. The innkeeper glanced at the sword, his grin disappearing, and vanished into the kitchen.

Vesth frowned again and turned, finding that Keliter had already found a table, keeping his back in the corner and facing the door. Vesth joined him, sitting so he could also watch the door and the hall that led to the kitchen, keeping his sword on the outside of the table in case he needed it.

"I do not like this place." He said quietly. Keliter nodded his agreement.

"The people here are... troubled somehow. I suspect it is our proximity to the Telatian wastes and the Temple of Water. It likely draws the spirits from the wastes and twists the minds of those sensitive enough to hear them." Vesth recalled the Dragon Tiamat mentioning the spirits in the wastes.

"I am beginning to feel it wise not to stay the night."

"And yet you payed for a room?" Keliter asked. Vesth shrugged.

"It would be suspicious not to. I don't want anyone to think we are leaving right away. If they did, they may rush to make a move and cause trouble. This way, we might slip away unnoticed." Keliter eyed the door, and someone shuffled quickly away.

"In any case, we must stay until nightfall. Your companion arrives as the moon reaches it's peak." Vesth watched the innkeeper come back from the kitchen, and start polishing his mugs again, his grin returning.

"Then we wait until the moon rises."

2

Chapter Two

Segine and Nysisset rode next to Brother Aegis and the other captains of the forward command. Nysisset was obviously very tired, which made her irritable, and Segine noticed that the other captains wisely gave her a wide berth.

"Will you make it to the mountains?" He asked carefully.

"Of course I will." She answered snappishly. Segine watched her eyes fade between dark and light shades of violet as she fought to keep her power flowing in even beats.

Two nights before, when they had used the silver cage to seal the amulet, she had collapsed as her power beat furiously and then stopped altogether. It started again the following night as the Dark Moon rose and she became feverish until the sun rose the following morning. She was still suffering, but her power was settling now and she insisted that she would be back to normal before the next night.

Segine gave her space, but made sure she was within arms reach should he need to keep her from toppling from her saddle.

Hundreds of soldiers marched in ranks behind them, keeping perfect time with their commanders. Segine was relieved that the soldiers of the brotherhood had at least been taught how to march.

"What do you expect from our coming battles?" Brother Aegis asked. He did not speak too softly, but Segine recognized that he had spoken only loudly enough for him to hear so as not to disturb Nysisset.

"I cannot be sure. I know that High Priest Borsa commands the Nibilus and Basilisk. I have also seen magic users at his beck and call, though they were slain by Master Solidus so I could not say how many more he commands. He is also certain to have others like himself, hosts to demons who can wield great power. But again the only one I have seen in person, aside from Borsa himself, was also slain by Master Solidus. Though that one did speak of others who were hunting the Alenon mages." Brother Aegis nodded and considered everything quietly.

"Considering the worst possibility, do you think our force is enough to handle the battle?" Segine looked over at Brother Aegis with a stony expression.

"I do not. The soldiers of the brotherhood are inexperienced and only barely proficient. They have learned their drills well enough, and in battle know to follow orders without question, but they are far from experts in any weapon disciplines. Coming up against any well trained soldier they will stand little chance. We will be better off once we join the armies of Laytrow and Hortaal, but they may not be sufficient. I am sorry to say that my kin, Though skilled in one on one combat, have little to no real battle experience. Gentry I think will fair far better, as they constantly contend with the sea and pirates. And Hortaal has been plagued with raiders for the past few years and will have some experience. On top of that some of the finest Swordsmen in Galbrea are in the Hortaal army and are led by an experienced commander." Brother Aegis nodded.

"Out of all the other commanders I would trust only High King Morien Toriel with the command of my troops. So you think we have no hope in a battle?" Segine considered his words carefully.

"With what knowledge I have of both sides, we do not stand any chance at all. However, I know that Master Solidus would not send us into a conflict that we had no chance of winning. Not unless it allowed for others to succeed where we cannot. In either instance, it is basic military strategy and I am willing to do my part. Besides," Brother Aegis glanced across at Segine from the corner of his eye.

"I do not think we have all the pieces. It is like playing a game where the pieces are covered and we are only being shown the board a little at a time. Right now some of the board remains covered, we do not know what other pieces are in play. Maybe there are others, such as the companions we were separated from, who will be powerful enough to sway the battle if they join us." They rode on for several more minutes, the only sound being the marching of the soldiers.

"What if I could give you an advantage?" Brother Aegis slowed his mount to ride even with Segine.

"Be careful what you plan to do Old Man." Nysisset grumbled. Segine's brow furrowed.

"What do you mean? What kind of advantage?" Brother Aegis rode on silently for a few moments before replying.

"Within the Human body there are Gates. Barriers that hold back the tides of our strength and limit us so we do not destroy ourselves."

"Dangerous to open, especially for humans." Nysisset added. She seemed to be speaking without thought.

"We have successfully opened the gates of several humans, giving them greater strength and agility. Making them strong enough to fight those few magic users who have tried to cause trouble since the Purge."

"It tears at the body, causes pain and strain that increases each time the gates are opened." Nysisset somehow followed the conversation while seemingly oblivious to everything else.

"We use keys to reduce the stress."

"Irrelevant." Nysisset turned slightly to gaze at the two men. "A key simply makes the opening easier. The strain remains the same." Brother Aegis frowned.

"Vesth has had his gates opened." Nysisset scoffed.

"His gate were ripped open by force. Even I could tell that his power leaked from his gates and caused great pain any time he moved. By now I suspect that Master Solidus has reshaped your seal and repaired the damage to Vesth's first gate." Brother Aegis looked back at Segine.

"There are risks involved and it will be painful any time you open your gates, but opening them will give you strength and dexterity that surpasses any normal soldier. The decision is yours, but keep in mind that you yourself said that, as we are, we do not stand a chance in the coming battles." Segine looked at Brother Aegis and then at Nysisset. Her eyes no longer faded between colors and her gaze was sharp. Segine considered things carefully, weighing his options, and finally made a decision.

"I am sorry Brother Aegis. But my gut tells me there is a different way to handle this matter. As generous as your offer is, I must decline." Brother Aegis glanced at Nysisset with something akin to annoyance and nodded. He tapped his reigns and urged his horse forward to the head of the column. Segine looked at Nysisset for several moments before speaking.

"Was that wise? We need all the strength we can muster." Nysisset nodded and urged her horse closer to Segine's and leaned in to whisper in his ear.

"Within you there is a potential. There is a better way." This said, she pulled back and returned to her moody trance, riding a few paces away. Segine felt as if he did not like what she had in mind any more than the suggestion from Brother Aegis.

The rest of the march was made in silence, the army making good time and coming within several miles of the Southwestern Gate as the sun began to set.

"Make camp here for the night. We will finish the march to the Gate when the sun rises on the marrow." Brother Aegis did not spare a glance to Segine or Nysisset, but instead directed the soldiers in erecting the tents and pavilions.

"Be sure to set watch fires around the camp and keep them fueled." Segine told the men under his direct command. Brother Aegis glanced questioningly at him.

"The last time I traveled the plains we were hounded by Nibilus." Segine explained. "I would rather keep them at arms length if we can." Brother Aegis nodded and continued to direct the soldiers. Segine directed the soldiers under his command to construct their tent and Nysisset disappeared inside once it was standing.

Segine made sure there were watch fires set around the camp at regular intervals to ensure there were no gaps in the light cast. As he worked, he felt his eyes being drawn again and again towards the Serpent Tongue mountains. He could see great clouds of dust forming across the mountains in Telatia, and what seemed almost like a faint glow coming from beneath.

"Sir Segine." The voice brought him back to the present.

"Yes? What is it?" The soldier saluted.

"Lady Nysisset calls for you." Segine nodded and dismissed the soldier, turning towards his tent. By the time he came into view of the tent, he knew something was off.

Nysisset stood outside the door, motioning for him to hurry. He quickened his stride and quickly reached her, opening his mouth to ask her what was wrong. She quickly placed a finger against his lips and glanced around to make sure no one was near.

"Tiamat has sent a minion to speak with us." Segine frowned, and Nysisset held open the tent flap for him to enter. He stepped inside to find a small figure only a few inches tall, wreathed in flames, standing in the center of the tent. Nysisset followed and looked down at the small creature.

"Why has Lord Tiamat sent you here? We were to make camp at the mouth of his cavern in two days time, could this not have waited?" The imp looked up at her and spoke in a surprisingly gruff voice.

"Lord Tiamat sends word. A presence has entered his domain, tainted with chaos."

"A demon then?" Nysisset asked. The imp nodded.

"A host, powerful, with little to no human presence left. It was traveling this way last we saw." Segine's frown deepened with each passing word.

"That sounds much like the Host that we encountered at the foot of the mountains before the Blood Moon Cycle." The Imp nodded.

"I was unable to make the connection, since Master Solidus dispensed with the creature quickly, but Lord Tiamat said as much."

"So then it is likely one of the hosts sent to hunt the Alenon Mages." Nysisset grumbled. The imp shrugged.

"I only know what Lord Tiamat commanded me to convey." Nysisset nodded, still grumbling.

"Very well, return to your master and inform him that we shall deal with the situation and return to his cavern per our instructions." The imp nodded.

"So long, hope you don't die." With this, the imp burst into flame and vanished.

"We have little time to waste, and we are not prepared to handle a demon host." Nysisset said, turning to Segine. "The soldiers are too weak, you don't have the power to fight a host, and I am not yet fully recovered."

"Then what do we do? Should we inform Brother Aegis and have the camp move on to the Great Gate? The armies there may be better equipped to fight." Nysisset shook her head.

"I doubt we have time to mobilize the camp, and the old man is too proud of his Soldiers to think they could be defeated by a single enemy."

"Then what do we do?" Segine repeated, waiting for the answer he knew he was not going to like.

"There is only one thing we can do if we want to survive this encounter without undue loss."

"The potential you spoke of before." Nysisset nodded.

"You have a rare potential to handle Lord Khornal's power." Segine shook his head.

"I will not give in to evil."

"Be silent and listen before you make judgment." Nysisset berated him. Segine flinched at the harsh tone in her voice.

"Lord Khornal is the Deity of Evil. That means he rules over all things that become evil or are considered part of the Darkness of this world. It does not mean that everything his power touches becomes evil. His most potent powers come from the darkness of this world, without which there would be no light. If you want to survive a fight with a demon host you will not be able to rely on your sword alone." Segine growled as he struggled within himself.

"Why should I choose to take on the Darkness instead of accepting Brother Aegis's offer?" Nysisset growled, holding up her hand, the tattoo on the side of her neck coming alive and traveling down her arm, darkening her hand, and forming a blade around her fingertips.

"The Nine Gates are fueled by your life force. The more you use them the shorter your life becomes and the weaker your body gets, forcing you to rely more and more on the Gates for strength. The darkness flows from every part of the world, it is always around you and Lord Khornal's blessing draws it's power from the world around you and your natural strength. It only enhances what you already have." Segine grumbled, looking for reasons to argue.

"But how are we going to get this 'Blessing'. We are too far from the Mercury Mountains to ask for such a thing." Nysisset moved like a blur, grabbing Segine's arm and clamping her darkened hand around his forearm. Segine felt his skin burn, and pain traveled up his arm into his shoulder and neck. Black mist roiled around Nysisset's hand, and before Segine could pull away, she pulled her hand across his arm, leaving a dark trail behind.

The shadowy smear twisted and writhed, pulling at Segine until it formed two crossing lines twisting down his arm to his wrist. Segine grasped his arm, fighting away the pain. Nysisset spoke, sounding tired.

"You will borrow my power tonight. If you decide you are not too good to accept the help of Great Khornal, then at another time perhaps we will meet with Master Khornal in person to discuss receiving your own blessing. I will hear no argument until this night is through, so bite your tongue." Segine growled, angry for having the decision forced onto him, and vowing to remove the mark on his arm as soon as he was able.

"Very well, we will do it your way but we must warn the camp that there is danger. I do not wish to worry about protecting them while I fight this threat." Nysisset nodded, seeming to approve of his attitude, which annoyed Segine further. Turning in place, Nysisset left the tent heading toward the main pavilion.

Segine watched her go and then doubled over, arm pressed against his chest. With every fiber of his body he wanted to scream. From pain, from frustration, from his own failings and being unable to force himself to make decisions.

"Try not to make things worse by fighting it." Segine

jumped, not having heard anyone enter the tent, but was not surprised to see an image of Master Solidus standing near him.

"I did not want this." Solidus nodded.

"Understandable. You were raised in a time and place where you are expected to handle everything using your own physical power. Normally that is a philosophy I would encourage." Segine grumbled.

"Then why must I endure this? Why can you not fight this threat like you did before?" Solidus frowned.

"I cannot do everything for you. There are other places and tasks I must attend to right now. Besides, how is relying on my power any different from relying on your own?" Segine stared at the floor.

"This power is evil."

"Wrong." Segine looked up at Solidus, frowning deeply.

"It is from the Deity of Evil, how could it not be?" Solidus shook his head.

"There is no such thing as evil power. You have darkness flowing through you now. Darkness is a source of power. Evil is not power it is action, emotion, intention. It is what you choose to do with your power that makes it good or evil. If that power was truly evil, it would have stayed sealed in the Mercury Mountains."

"But Nysisset was sealed to you." Segine argued.

"Irrelevant." Solidus countered, staring down the knight. "She was sealed to me so that her body could leave the mountains without destruction. If she was truly evil she would still have been pulled back into the mountains when she tried to leave. Very few of Lord Khornal's servants are purely evil. They were raised to do as their Master ordered, and their attitudes shaped to reflect his own, but any one of them could walk out of the Mercury Mountains right now if they truly had a change of heart and wished to do good." Segine continued to frown, the marks on his arm feeling like fire.

"Is there truly no other way?" Solidus nodded.

"Even if you had chosen to have your gates unlocked, it takes great skill and innate talent to control it. You do not have time to train your body and mind to control your life force. It is the same skill and training required to control magic, and that can take years, or even decades." Segine grumbled.

"Then how do I control this?" He asked, raising his marked arm.

"You do not." Solidus stated. "It is a part of you now. It's power reflects your actions. If you attack, it will attack with you. If you defend, it will protect you. If you become angry, it will be fueled by your rage, and if you are calm it's actions will be smooth and precise. If you wish it to be a controlled power then you yourself must be controlled. So I suggest you remember your discipline, Sir Knight." Segine thought carefully, then let his mind enter a state of void.

The pain in his arm and shoulder faded away, and he looked at the two marks on his arm blankly. They no longer seemed to look so dark and menacing.

"What does Lord Khornal want in return for using the power he grants?" Segine asked, as he felt the dark power flowing through him in even tides.

"Lord Khornal asks for nothing in return for his power. If you can make your way to him on your own and ask for it, he will grant it." Segine looked at Solidus letting his arm fall limply at his side.

"He won't ask for anything dishonorable in return?" Solidus shook his head.

"It is his way of spreading his evil. He knows that power can be a corrupting influence. Men are weak to power, give a man strength and he will abuse it. The more it is abused, the more twisted a man can become. However, if your will is strong and your heart is pure you have no fear of being corrupted by any power, no matter it's source." Segine stood, quietly thinking, and Solidus waited patiently.

"What must I expect from the Demon Host coming here?" Solidus looked off towards the east.

"His power is chaotic, uncontrolled. His physical motions will be unpredictable, and difficult to follow. His human essence is all but gone and only the demon remains. But that is your advantage. Demons are creatures of chaos. They do not naturally exist with a physical form and it is difficult for them to control. However, do not underestimate them, They are far stronger than humans and can move like lightning. His magic will burst from him in waves, so it would be best if you could fight him as far from others as you can. He should focus entirely on you once you show him your power." Segine nodded, feeling defeated and excepting how things were going to be. Solidus seemed to read his mind.

"If you want to be able to help and support your companions, you are going to need to find some source of strength." Segine met Solidus's gaze.

"My... companions." Solidus nodded.

"They all have power and strength of their own, but if they are ever in trouble who will they be able to turn to for help? I cannot always be around to help you, my duties are endless and even I need rest from time to time. It would be best to gain strength and power of your own so that they may fall back on you whenever the need may arise, would it not? And where else will you find a power that comes at no personal cost to you and requires no real training to use?" Segine nodded slowly.

"Then I have no other choice. I trust you, Master Solidus, And against all my better judgment I trust Nysisset. No matter how hard I try, I cannot see her as evil. Cruel sometimes, perhaps, but not evil." Solidus nodded with a slight smile.

"As I said, her personality was tailored to match that of Lord Khornal. But she has a great capacity for kindness and empathy when she chooses. It Is for that reason that Khornal made her his Angel of Death, the farrier of souls to his heaven realm. That is also why she tries to push you so hard. You and Rielle are the first people she has ever cared about and considered as true companions. And since she got attached to and lost Tiasia, she has vowed never to let another of her companions die." Segine felt a ping in his gut and his heart ached at the mention of the little girl from the Moon Witch Forest.

"Then I will accept this burden." He looked at the marks on his arm again and made a tight fist. "At least until this prediction is past, I will do everything I can to protect them. Even if it means asking the Deity of Evil himself for the power to do so." Solidus smiled.

"A man who can set aside his pride for the sake of others is already strong enough to endure any hardship." Solidus placed his transparent hand on Segine's shoulder. "There are parts yet left for you to play. When this fight is over go to Tiamat's cave, everything you need to do will be explained as best it can be." Segine nodded, placing his fist over his heart in salute.

"Thank you, Master Solidus." Solidus nodded and looked at the tent door.

"Nysisset, my presence here will have made the host wary. But that will not hold him at bay for long. Make sure the rest of the camp is as out of the way as they can be." Segine looked over and found Nysisset waiting quietly in the doorway. She nodded.

"As you say, Master Solidus." Solidus nodded and then vanished. Segine straightened himself and walked over to the door, waiting for some sort of scolding from Nysisset. She waited silently for a few moments then reached up and carefully pulled the amulet from around her neck, holding it out for Segine.

"Put this on, it will increase your strength, and give your power focus." Segine looked at the small black stone in it's silver cage, then carefully accepted it. As the amulet left her hand Nysisset swayed slightly. Segine reached out and placed a steadying hand on her shoulder. Instead of pulling back and scolding him as he expected, she temporarily leaned against his arm.

"Thank you." She spoke quietly. Segine swallowed.

"Will you be alright?" Nysisset nodded.

"It is still very near the Dark Moon Cycle. As the moon rises I will regain some of my strength. But you do not have time to worry about that right now." She pushed away from his arm carefully and stood on her own.

"The host will come directly from the east, it would be best to wait for him on that side of the camp." She turned to leave and Segine, without really knowing why, reached out and caught her hand. She paused looking back over her shoulder at Segine.

"Yes, Knight?" Segine fumbled for a moment and then spoke.

"I am sorry for becoming angry with you. I let my own weakness get the better of me and I should not have spoken as I did." Nysisset looked Segine up and down.

"You are only human after all. You cannot be perfect." Segine blinked a few times, unable to think of anything else to say. Nysisset smiled softly at him.

"We have much to do this night." She lightly squeezed his hand and then headed towards the center of the camp.

"Be careful." She said as she went. Segine stood quietly staring at his hand for several moments before balling it into a tight fist. He pushed past the entrance of the tent and headed towards the east side of camp, drawing his sword as he walked.

"I swear." He said aloud. "I swear I will fight." He raised his sword and slid his open hand across the blade, leaving a thin trail of blood behind.

"I will fight, and I will protect her until my dying breath." His bleeding hand clamped tightly onto his sword arm. When he removed it, a bloody hand print stained his arm.

"By this mark of battle I swear, never will it be broken." His features hardened, his hand tightened on his sword, and the last thing that went through his mind as it was enveloped by the void was the image of Nysisset's soft smile.

3

Chapter Three

Vesth watched the guards walk into the inn and immediately knew there would be trouble.

"Is it time?" He asked quietly. Keliter's gaze never left the guards.

"Nearly." Vesth felt his shoulders tighten.

"I am afraid you will have to come with us." One of the guards said.

"Is there a problem?" Keliter asked. The second guard scowled.

"Your kind is not welcome here." Vesth watched them eye their weapons.

"I am afraid I do not understand." Vesth stated, keeping eye contact with the guards. "We have caused no trouble, we payed for a room here and planned to spend the night before heading out in the morning." one of the guards hefted his spear in both hands and the second placed his hand on the hilt of his sword.

"You are not welcome here. You will come with us quietly or in pieces."

"It is not wise to threaten strangers." Keliter said quietly. Vesth tapped one hand on the table as a signal to stay still.

"If we are not welcome, then we will leave. I will get my money back for the room and we will leave without trouble." The guard with the sword drew his weapon.

"It is too late for that. You should never have set foot in town to begin with." Vesth sighed.

"That simply won't do." Before they could even blink, Vesth left his seat, drawing his sword and disarming the guard. He knocked the man back and kicked his sword beneath the table and aimed the tip of his sword at the guard's eyes. He heard the second guard hit the floor and scramble to his feet as Keliter joined Vesth with the man's spear.

"I would hope that the men who claim to protect their town would be a bit more respectful." Both guards glared at them angrily.

"You will regret this." The first one said, eyeing the point of Vesth's sword.

"No." Vesth stated, tipping his sword so that the Dragon on his blade was plainly visible. "I won't." The second guard's eyes widened and he pulled his companion toward the door.

"You should have come quietly." He said, then turned and quickly left, the other guard in tow. Vesth returned his sword to it's scabbard and glanced at the innkeeper, who was trying his best not to be noticed behind the counter.

"We will not require your room tonight." He stated. The

innkeeper nodded and glanced at something below the bar. He jumped as the guard's spear embedded itself in the counter directly above where he had been looking.

"Make a move for it, and you might lose something important." Keliter said, an emotionless smile on his face. The innkeeper nodded nervously.

"Feel free to keep the gold I payed for our room." Vesth said, as he walked towards the doorway. "Perhaps you could use it to repair your counter top." The innkeeper watched them go, then pulled a small hand crossbow from under the bar and set it on the counter.

Vesth and Keliter slipped away quietly, drawing the hoods of their cloaks up over their heads. Vesth untied their horses and then tied Keliter's horse to his own saddle. He motioned to the road that led out of town and tapped his horse's side. It bobbed it's head and then set off down the road, the other horse in tow.

Vesth turned and nodded to Keliter who slipped down an alley, Vesth followed closely behind. They crept through the town quietly, keeping to the shadows, making their way towards the center of town. Keliter stopped at the corner of a building and looked up at the sky.

"The Moon is at it's peak. The time is here." He whispered.

As if to confirm the words Keliter had spoken, several guards ran by, their spears raised anxiously. Vesth and Keliter waited a few seconds and then slipped out onto the street and followed them.

Winding in and out of buildings, they followed until the guards entered the town square. After a moment's pause the two men made their way through a narrow alley, and turned a darkened corner to come into full view of the town center. Vesth froze as he saw the scene laid out before him.

Rielle stood in the center of the town square, sword drawn, her eyes crazed. Her skin was pale in the faint moonlight, and her face was gaunt with hunger. The villagers stood around her, watching in fear, as she lashed out at any who moved. Several guards stood between her and the people, trying to keep her at bay with their spears. Vesth clenched his hands and reached for his own sword. A dark hand grasped his wrist.

"You cannot stop her." Vesth growled and tried to shake off the hand.

"Let go of me Keliter, I have to try." The hand did not loosen it's grasp.

"You don't have the strength to beat her. You cannot open enough gates to match her yet." Vesth glanced back at the Telatian in mild surprise.

"What would you know." Keliter met his gaze coldly.

"I know that you would need to open at least your fourth gate to match the speed of the Cloak of the Wind. As of now you can only control your strength up to the third. I also know that you are likely the only one who can get to the last remaining scraps of her sanity. But in order for you to speak to her, she would have to be subdued." Vesth once again pulled at the hand that held him.

"Then let me do this."

"No." Keliter commanded, pulling him back into the alley. Then the Telatian stepped forward, drawing the long knife from his belt, the rearing dragon on the blade brightly reflecting the moon and stars.

"Let me." He stepped out into the light cast by the torches

many people were holding and Vesth followed, drawing his sword, his eyes on Keliter's dragon blade.

"I suggest you all stand back if you do not want to die." Keliter stated coldly. Several people nearby jumped, causing Rielle to twist and violently swing her sword. The villagers quickly moved out of the way, and the guards jumped in to bar the path.

"They must be the ones who brought the crazed witch." One guard said. Vesth growled, causing the villagers to step even further away.

"If that is the case, then we are also the only ones who can make her leave." Keliter said. "Again, if you don't want to die, I suggest you stand back." The guards fidgeted uncomfortably. The motion caught Rielle's attention and she leapt at them. Keliter moved faster than the eye could follow, sparks flying as his blade crossed with hers. The guards, seeing an opportunity, lunged at Keliter's exposed back. Their spears splintered as Vesth slipped in front of them and knocked them all back with one powerful swing of his sword. Vesth skidded to a stop and raised his sword above his head with both hands.

"The next man who tries to interfere will lose his life." The guards fell back, fearful of the rage that showed clearly on Vesth's face.

"Make this quick, Keliter." Keliter nodded.

"I am sorry Lady Rielle." He said. He half turned and planted a solid kick to her abdomen, sending her sliding backwards across the hard ground. Her gaze seemed to focus slightly as she watched him.

"That is right, your name is Rielle." Rielle's head tilted slightly to one side, lowering her sword. Keliter raised his knife.

"Here it comes." He muttered. Vesth nodded, not taking his gaze from the guards still standing before him. Rielle slowly began to sway, back and forth. As she swayed, thin wisps of white haze seemed to dance around her. Keliter slowly reversed his grip on the knife and lowered his stance.

"Cloaked in Wind, blessed of Sidhe, show me your strength, Student of Solidus." Rielle twisted and gripped her sword in both hands, took one step, and vanished from sight. Keliter moved like a flash of lightning, a sound like the crack of thunder echoing through the buildings as their blades met. A blast of wind pushed at Vesth's back and drove back the villagers, putting out many of their torches.

Vesth noticed something as another clash sounded behind him. A figure, standing almost out of sight, alone on the road, watching as the duel raged. The figure's simple brown cloak waved in the wind, his brown hood covering his eyes and most of his face, but a full gray beard trailed from it, pinned against his chest from the wind. The figure noticed Vesth watching, and Vesth's jaw set as the figure grinned and nodded to him. Vesth nodded in return.

"Keliter, finish this now." He felt Keliter come back to back with him.

"She could be injured if we are not careful."

"As long as she is alive and whole. We are out of time." Vesth felt Keliter nod. The air grew heavy around them and Vesth recognized that Keliter was opening more of his Gates." Wind buffeted Vesth when he moved and he immediately heard a strange noise, similar to the rasp of a sharpening stone, followed by a hum. A sword blade landed, point down, in the dirt near Vesth's feet, severed from it's hilt. A quiet thud told Vesth that Keliter had knocked Rielle unconscious.

One last look at the figure down the road and Vesth quickly turned and helped Keliter lift Rielle onto his shoulders. The guards began to tighten their circle around them, spears pointed at their hearts.

"The next time someone visit's your town you may not be so lucky." Vesth said menacingly. "If you do not change your ways, eventually someone will lose their life here." Vesth heard a wordless shout as the guards charged them, then a bright flash filled his vision and he was standing in the long grass near the base of the mountain.

"I appreciate your intervention, Master Delgorin." Vesth heard the old man chuckle.

"Well, you seemed to be in a spot of trouble." Vesth nodded and helped Keliter carefully lay Rielle down on the grass. Vesth placed one hand on her forehead and found her to be feverish.

"Do you know if there is water nearby?" Delgorin nodded.

"There is a creek nearby that flows down the mountain to the sea." Vesth stood and placed his pack beside Rielle.

"Please point me in the right direction." Delgorin chuckled but shook his head.

"No, I think it would be better if I go. It would be best if you stayed here and watched over Rielle. She has had it rough over the past few days. Your new friend and I can take care of the water." Vesth looked at Keliter, who nodded.

"You tend to miss Rielle, if she wakes it would be best if it was to a familiar face." Vesth nodded and knelt back down and began searching his pack for anything he could use.

"Come with me young one." Delgorin said, motioning to

Keliter. Keliter followed Delgorin without question, following the curve of the hills. Once they had lost sight of Vesth and Rielle, Delgorin spoke again.

"I assume you haven't told him who you really are." Keliter didn't seem surprised by the question.

"It would have broken his trust, and I wouldn't have been able to help him if he didn't trust me." Delgorin glanced back at him.

"Rielle will recognize you once she wakes." Keliter nodded.

"I suspect as much, but the ambassador has always been level headed. I think she will likely question me thoroughly before making a decision on whether or not to trust me. She may never fully trust me, which is fine, but I am not tainted like others who were in the service of the High Priest. I was sure to make myself useful enough that the High Priest would have no need to install a Demon of any kind inside me." Delgorin once again focused on the path they were walking.

"Is that so? Why would you now choose to work against the High Priest?" Keliter took a moment to consider before speaking.

"I was once very devout to my beliefs. I was raised within a cult that took pride in twisting humans into monsters. I was intelligent, more so than the others within the cult, and I could see they had no purpose in what they did. They followed a system they no longer understood, they simply followed because they had been told to follow.

Our travels eventually led us to the gates of Tyr' Anon. I was still fairly young, but I could immediately feel something out of place there. Something different than every other city we had been in. I searched the city and eventually found myself standing outside the temple doors. It was not hard for me to sneak inside and look around.

I found myself deep within the lowest levels of the temple. I could hear the familiar screams and shouts of torture and followed them to a grand sight. A large room with an altar of black stone. All around it were symbols and diagrams, many of which I recognized as the symbols the cultists used in their rituals." Delgorin grunted.

"It is a wonder you were not twisted by the chaos there. Even those of us who have trained to protect ourselves from it can often find it difficult." Keliter nodded.

"I did not know it, but I had had my second gate opened at that time and it was never shut. The flow of energy somehow prevented the chaos from finding anywhere within me to settle and corrupt." Delgorin grunted again.

"I see. Continue." Keliter subconsciously scratched his chin before speaking again.

"I waited for several hours, and I was finally rewarded for my patience. A young man was carried in, bound and gagged, and bolted to the altar. A man in black robes stood beside them and began speaking twisted words that caused the young man to arch in agony. Later I found out he was having a demon sealed inside of him.

It was so very much like what the cultists did and I felt, as I watch the ceremony, that this person, whoever he may be, was following a more complete method than the cultists. Most importantly, he seemed to have a reason for doing it. When everything was done he turned and looked directly at me in my hiding spot, and asked me if I had enjoyed watching. I stepped forward, unafraid, and stated my pleasure at seeing a ceremony performed with true purpose rather than for the pleasure. I became that man's personal servant from that moment on." Delgorin walked on in silence for several minutes until they came to the narrow creek bed.

"If you were so impressed with the High Priests actions, then why now do you fight him?" Delgorin repeated his previous question. Keliter stared down into the water.

"Because I began to see the High Priest's purpose. I could see the threads that tied things together being undone around him. He believed that all existence was pain, and that he would cure that pain by making sure everything ceased to exist. I followed him because he still had purpose where before I had seen none.

But when he made the decision to destroy Tyr' Anon, rather than wait for the Blood Moon Cycle, I made the decision to leave his service. If he did not plan on inflicting as much pain as he could before ensuring his plan came to fruition, I might have still followed him. But, I cannot follow a man whose only purpose is to destroy the world because of a reason he himself causes. If his reasons persisted in spite of him, then I would have served him. But he wishes only to add to the pain in this world, seemingly to prove to himself that he is following the correct path." Delgorin nodded.

"I see. You have a clear mind for one your age. Perhaps Master Solidus was right in directing me to leave you be while you followed Vesth and Rielle." Keliter looked back over his shoulder the way they had come.

"Vesth and Rielle. They too seem to move with a purpose." Delgorin nodded once again and reached down with a small flask and filled it from the creek.

"Their purpose is to protect the balance of the world. They fight to protect the people of the world, those they care about, and the very world itself. They do not think of selfish gain, nor do they seek glory or honor. They fight because they believe that it is the right thing to do." Keliter looked down at the old man.

"Because they believe it is right?" Delgorin nodded and handed him the filled flask.

"Sometimes the only purpose you need is that you believe in something. Even if it is merely believing you can continue on living. A purpose for living is not simply some thing that is out in the world for you to find, it is something you decide to live for on your own." Keliter tied the flask to his back and pulled an empty one from his belt.

"But does your Deity not give you purpose?" Delgorin nodded and stood up with a grunt.

"Indeed she does young lad, But I still have to choose to accept the purpose she gave me. I have to decide each day whether or not I want to continue to live for that purpose. Not everyone can accept what they are asked to do.

It is for that reason that Alenon was thrust beneath the waves. It is for that reason only four of us remain. We were the only ones who chose to listen and do as we were asked. We trusted in our Deity to guide us. Our purpose in life is not just some simple task to perform. Our purpose for living is to serve her with all our strength, regardless of what task we are given. We have chosen that purpose, and we will continue to serve until we are no longer needed." Keliter stood quietly, thinking to himself as he turned the flask in his hands over and over.

Delgorin watched him for several seconds then, with a

mischievous glint in his eye, he pushed Keliter towards the creek, nearly knocking him in.

"Well, fill that flask then and lets hurry back and check on Vesth and miss Rielle."

* * *

Vesth unbundled the soft velvety cloak he had found in his bag and placed it over Rielle. He tore a few strips of scrap cloth and carefully wrapped them around Rielle's scratched arms and hands. He examined the hilt of her broken sword and, finding it irreparable, tossed it aside. Then, being unable to think of anything else to do, he sat quietly beside Rielle looking down at her pale face.

He felt like he should be more worried or afraid for her in some way, but he sat idly by, his mind as quiet as his surroundings. At one time he felt as if there was a presence with them, but when he looked around he could only see barren ground and spars grass. He remained quiet and vigilant until Keliter and Delgorin returned with the water.

Vesth noticed a strange expression cross Delgorin's face when they came into sight. At first he ignored it and gently lifted Rielle's head as Keliter carefully tipped one of the flasks so she might drink.

They decided to make camp for the night and Keliter set to the task of finding what small brush and twigs he could to start a fire. Vesth began laying out bed rolls and Delgorin helped him lift Rielle and move her to one of the beds. It was then that Vesth noticed the strange expression on the old man's face again.

"Does something bother you, Master Delgorin?" Delgorin

spared Vesth a glance and looked back down at Rielle, seeming more worn and serious than normal.

"Where did you find this cloak?" Vesth examined the soft cloak he had wrapped around Rielle.

"I think Master Solidus gave it to me before I left Terramine. What of it?" Vesth knew this was something he would normally be wary of, but looking down at the cloak he still felt calm. Delgorin quietly watched Rielle.

"So that is why he was not worried for her safety." Vesth watched the old man carefully.

"Is there something special about this cloak?" Delgorin half chuckled, though he obviously didn't find it particularly amusing.

"I doubt you grasp the gravity of what was given to you. This is the cloak Master Solidus wore into battle when he Destroyed Telatia." Even the calm that had settled around them could not cushion the sudden shock Vesth felt. Delgorin continued.

"Fifteen hundred years ago Tyr' Anon had been overrun by Demons. They were spreading throughout Telatia, corrupting the oasis and fairies as they went. It finally came to a point that it was no longer possible to reclaim the land or its living creatures, and Master Solidus was forced to destroy nearly all of Telatia, banishing everything into the chaos in order to bring everything back into balance.

To protect himself from the touch of the chaos as he tore open reality, he wore a cloak enchanted and blessed by our Deity in Alenon. The cloak was formed from the very soul of his predecessor, The Matriarch. She dwelled within the cloak and protected him from the whisperings of the chaos, and consoled him as he was forced to take so many lives." Vesth stared down at the cloak.

"The Matriarch, I have heard that name before." Delgorin nodded.

"One of the first Balance Mages. The Patriarch and The Matriarch were the first humans to be given the ability to sense the balance of the world, and the only ones who were ever born with the power to freely manipulate the world as the six Deities did.

Solidus and Marina are the only ones old enough to remember them. Master Solidus studied with them for many years as he trained to become a Balance Mage, and Marina lost her parents at a young age and was raised in the temple where she saw them on rare occasions. But they were taken by the Six Deities, before Marina was even fully grown, to complete a task in the Heaven Realm. It can only be assumed that they were able to complete their task and were returned to the mortal realm in one form or another to continue shaping the world until the end time comes." Vesth thought silently for a moment before speaking.

"So if the cloak here represents the soul of The Matriarch, then that would mean that Rielle's sword is..." Delgorin nodded.

"The sword houses the soul of her partner, The Patriarch. Master Solidus knew they would both be needed by the end days. So when he went into exile in the Mercury Mountains he began forging a sword from the metal that flows from the ancient mercury spring that gave the mountains their name.

Then, with the aid of Necrotic Dracolich Khornal, they reached out to the Heaven Realm and called The Patriarch's soul into the sword where Solidus sealed it and then passed the blade onto Marina to finalize the seals and shape the sword to perfection." Vesth felt himself slowly sitting down. Delgorin watched him soberly.

"Rielle is as safe as she can be for now. The Patriarch cuts into the void itself and allows the voices of the chaos to be heard, but the Matriarch will now protect miss Rielle from those whispers. That is not to say that things will be easy. It will still be a while before she recovers again, and she will need to be carefully tended to.

I would suggest you stay here until she wakes and then start out towards the Temple of Water. If you take things slowly she should be mostly recovered by the time you arrive there. Afterwards Master Solidus has instructed me to point you back in the direction of Lord Tiamat's cave. More instructions will be waiting for you when you arrive there." Not waiting for Vesth to respond Delgorin turned and began walking away.

"You will hear miss Rielle talking to herself now and again from here on, do not worry for her. It is the voices of the Matriarch and Patriarch that she will now be able to hear, and they will be able to give her guidance in the same way Master Solidus did when he was housed in her mind." This said, Delgorin vanished into a thin wisp of dust, leaving Vesth to contemplate everything he had been told in the silence of the mountainside.

4

Chapter Four

Segine frowned at the man before him, his sword prepared to strike if the need arose.

"Are you the only one who dared to come to meet me?" The voice was mellow and smooth. "How very... sad." Segine continued to frown.

"I am the only one who will be necessary." The man's hood shifted as his head tipped to one side.

"Oh? That is an interesting assumption. I wonder what makes you believe that." Segine stood quietly, his mind all but a blank slate. The man tilted his head the other way.

"A man of few words? Then shall we speak with action instead?" Segine responded by leveling his sword at the man's heart. The man straightened and two wide, curved blades slid out of his long sleeves.

"We Dance." The man leapt at Segine, spinning in the air

like a whirlwind of blades. Segine stepped back, swinging his sword back and forth in wide arcs. Several times he heard his sword strike his opponent's blades, but he never managed to connect a solid hit.

The man swayed back and forth, lurching from side to side as he fought. Segine, many times, thought he would lose his footing and fall, but he always somehow managed to twist around and plant at least one limb on the ground to steady himself, slashing the air at random all the while.

The first shock wave caught Segine by surprise as the man spun, knocking Segine back and releasing a blast of energy. Segine quickly rolled back and onto one knee again, using his sword to block a second shock wave. Segine watched as the black mark on his arm raced across his hand and down the blade of his sword to deflect the energy.

"You have a strange sense about you." The man stated, twisting and turning his body until he was upright again.

"Your movements are calculated, perfect, without passion. You are keeping something of yourself locked away." Segine stood, squared his shoulders and took his sword in both hands.

"I am a knight, Self Control is of the highest priority. Passion is reserved for love and politics, it has no place on the battlefield." The man began to sway back and forth again.

"But control is so stifling, so painful, so constricting." The man's mellow voice almost began to take on an emotional tone. "Is it not better to loose all the bands that bind you, to let yourself free and reach the pinnacle of existence?" Segine quietly watched the man.

"You tell me, demon. You came to this world from the chaos, a place where nothing is controlled. You took on a human body, a physical and restrictive form. If it is so trouble-some, should you not simply return to the chaos?" The man paused a moment to consider.

"It is true that this body is weak, and a mere prison for my power." The man arched backwards until his head was nearly touching the ground, staring back towards Telatia.

"But the Great One who Bound us here will destroy us if we disobey. Rip us from the chaos and scatter our essence to the void." Segine tightened the grip on his sword.

"It sounds to me as if it is not the physical body you have that constricts and controls you." The man slowly stood upright, his two swords falling from his sleeves.

"I grow bored. I had hoped you would provide more en-tertainment, but you do not allow yourself to let go during battle." The man raised his arms slightly and his robe slid from his thin shoulders.

Segine felt a pang of horror. The man was deathly thin with only a thin pair of breeches tied tightly to him. His bones stood out clearly underneath his pale skin, his muscles clearly atro-phied to the point of non-existence. His stomach was wasted away to almost nothing and hip bones jutted out sharply to either side. But Segine's eyes were drawn again and again to the man's face.

Where his eyes and nose should have been were only smooth hollows covered in skin, as if he had never had facial features at all. All that remained to identify it as his face was a thin lipped mouth, filled with sharpened teeth.

Long black tendrils rose from his back and several began to sprout from his chest, twitching and writhing, only semi-solid as if made of smoke. Segine remembered the Host they had met on the night of the Blood Moon Cycle. The one who had stood, black tendrils sprouting like smoke from his back. The one who had killed Tiasia.

Segine felt an inkling of anger rise up within him. He clenched his teeth and tightened his grip on his sword. Immediately the black mark on his arm reacted, racing down his arm to his blade once again. This time it formed a sharp blade along the edge of his sword. The man swayed back and forth.

"What is this? I sense something within you now." His mouth parted in a wide grin that exposed his sharpened teeth.

"Maybe you are not the perfect stone I imagined you to be." Segine leapt at the man with a growl and tried to run him through. The man fell back and slipped beneath Segine's blade as if the ground had fallen out from under him. Segine dropped his heavy sword blade, hoping to catch the unprotected man with it's sharp edge.

The man twisted mid-fall and moved to one side, escaping the deadly attack. Segine felt four strong impacts all at once in front and back and against his right side. The blow knocked him off his feet and he felt the man's blades narrowly miss his face and head as he fell.

Segine hit the ground hard and hurriedly rolled to his feet, dropping into a low guard behind his sword just in time to intercept several more blows. He skidded back under the force of the attack and only just managed to retreat to a safe distance before he was overwhelmed. The man now swayed back and forth, his feet no longer touching the ground, supported by several black tendrils.

"As impressive as your human strength is, I am afraid I have no more time to spend fighting you. I have important tasks to perform." The man raised his arms and the black tendrils quivered.

"Good bye human." The black tendrils suddenly sharpened and shot at Segine like spears. Segine quickly raised his sword to defend and felt sharp pain lance through him as tendrils pierced his left shoulder and side. There was a loud sound, like a hammer striking an anvil, and Segine was thrown off his feet, falling to land heavily on his back.

"Impressive, I did not think your sword could take such a blow." The man said. Segine groaned as he turned his head to one side to look at his sword. To his surprise he could see a clearly defined crack running almost the full length down the center of his blade.

"Unfortunately you do not seem to have held up so well." Segine growled as he discovered he was unable to move his left arm.

"This time really will be good bye." The man stated, rising higher, his tendrils at the ready.

Then, the air became heavy. The world slowed around Segine and he found it becoming more difficult to breath. He closed his eyes, waiting for his end to come.

"*Giving up already are we?*" Segine heard the smooth voice sound clearly in his mind and his eyes flew open. All around him it seemed as if the world had frozen. Nothing moved, no sound was heard, even the quiet wind had come to a standstill. Segine managed to draw breath enough to speak.

"Who are you?" He felt, more than heard, the chuckle that answered him.

"*Was our first meeting so traumatizing to you that you cannot even remember my voice?*" Segine frowned, not able to think with any real clarity. He remembered gold and armor and fire, but he could not remember where he had seen them.

"I will give you a hint. You are currently traveling with something that belongs to me." Segine felt that the voice was amused. He could not think of anything he carried that he had not had before his journey began. He racked his brain for several moments before he was met by an image of jet black hair and violet eyes.

"Nysisset." He whispered.

"I don't know what she sees in you." The voice answered conversationally. *"I am certain it is not what I see, and I am also certain that she was acting in a moment of foolishness when she chose to divide herself to protect you."* Segine suddenly felt his throat grow tight.

"Necrotic Dracolich Khornal." Segine swore he could hear the Deity of Evil clapping.

"It took some time, but we got there." Segine tried to swallow the lump growing in his throat.

"Why are you choosing to speak with me now?" Segine could imagine the Deity sitting back in his great black throne, sipping his glass of wine.

"Well, simply put, you are about to die." Segine did not find the statement as shocking as he thought it should have been.

"If I am to die, what purpose would the Deity of Evil have to speak with me?" He heard the Deity sigh heavily.

"Well, it is my duty to ensure the cycles of life and death remain uninterrupted. It is I who decides whether or not a soul passes on or is reborn. However, I also have another reason for my visit. My servant Nysisset has grown quite fond of you and your other companions. I can't for the life of me decide why. Now,

if at all possible, I would like to get my servant back at some point. And if she could come back whole I would be all the more appreciative." Segine stared blankly at the night sky.

"What does that have to do with me?" He could feel the Deity chuckling again.

"My My, you are not good at following context, are you boy?" Segine could not disagree, so he sat quietly and listened. He felt a nod of approval.

"At least you have that going for you. There are two problems that stem from me allowing you to die. First, and foremost, you have a portion of Nysisset's power inside you. If you die, that portion of power will die with you and Nysisset will no longer have the strength to fight the enemy before you and survive." Segine nodded, looking at the demon host above him, suspended in time.

"That is a logical conclusion."

"The second problem is not." The Deity stated. *"Remember I told you she had grown fond of you and your other companions? She already lost one, and it chipped away at the wall she has built around her heart to protect herself from feeling. If you die as well that wall will crumble and her mind will likely break along with it."* Segine felt a jolt in his gut, as if he had been struck by lightning.

"I am sure you can see how that is a problem for me." Segine thought over everything he had heard for a few moments, grinding his teeth nervously for several seconds before forcing himself to make a decision.

"If I ask it of you, Great Khornal, would you grant me the power to defeat this enemy?" Segine felt as if the Deity was leaning back in his throne, scratching his chin thoughtfully.

"*That could be one solution to the problem at hand, But I seem to recall you not wanting any part of my power.*" Segine clenched his fist.

"I am a knight, raised to be the most righteous in the land, free from flaw. However, I know that I have also allowed it to blind me. I see everything in terms of black and white, Good and Evil." Segine felt the Deity grow more somber and he felt like a great weight was added to his chest.

"*And you see yourself on the side of Good, fighting Evil. Be careful you do not fall into the same trap as my dear Sister's Alenon. Just because something is Good, does not mean it cannot be used for great Evil.*" Segine nodded painfully.

"Master Solidus said something similar. Power is not evil, it is what is done with it that makes it Good or Evil. If you will grant me strength, no matter what it is, I can choose to use it for Good." Segine waited for a reply. What seemed like an eternity passed before he got one.

"*What do I get in return? What benefit do I have for giving my power to be used for Good?*"

"I will protect Nysisset." The Deity harumphed.

"*I can always make myself a new servant if I must. It is a tedious and time consuming process, but it is not difficult. I am afraid you will have to do better than that.*" Segine frowned.

"Does the Deity of Evil not grant power to those who come seeking it?" He felt the Deity wave his hand negligently.

"*In times past, yes. But those who came seeking my power were all easily corrupted by the power I gave them. They all fell to darkness and I gained servants in return. But this case is a bit different. How can I be sure that you will not simply use my power then discard it to the wayside when you decide you are through?"* Segine looked down at the bloody hand print on his arm.

"I swear, on my blood, that I will use the power I am given to protect Nysisset for as long as I live. I, Segine Memoria, will swear an oath before the Six Deities of Galbrea if it means I will be given the strength to protect her." Segine felt the Deity sit up in his throne.

"Memoria? Well now, I thought your bloodline was familiar to me." Segine felt a sinister smile in the back of his mind, then flinched as he felt the wounds in his shoulder and side knitting themselves together.

"I am convinced for now, Knight. I will grant you power for this one night. When you have finished your business at Tiamat's cave, have him send you to me and we will discuss a more permanent arrangement. Your blood oath will serve as your brand for now." Segine felt his left arm burn, much in the same way his right arm had when Nysisset passed her power onto him. The blood red hand print darkened to black and marks like stars appeared around it.

"Your sword is useless now. Discard it and fight without it if you do not wish it to break." Segine felt his hand grip his sword defensively.

"What would a Deity know of swords?" Segine felt the Deity's grin widen.

"You seem to forget that without us Deities, swords would not exist. Nor warriors to wield them. Your brand is your weapon now. It will act as you will it to act." Segine kept a tight grip on his sword. The Deity chuckled.

"As good as Taeldora Marina's work is, that is only a mediocre blade. It will not stand up to combat such as this. If you are

still not convinced that I know of what I speak, knight, keep this one fact in mind. I am the only one left in this world or the next who can go head to head in a duel with Pravin Solidus... and win." Segine jerked in surprise, a feeling like being rammed by a bull hitting him in the chest.

"*Happy hunting.*" The Deity's voice trailed away with a haunting laugh and Segine felt the world around him beginning to move again. Segine slowly stood, his sword slipping from his hand to the ground. The Host looked him up and down.

"Your wounds are gone. How are you able to do this?" Segine breathed deeply, feeling the weight of the black stone against his chest as it seemed to fill him with strength.

"I would know your name before we end this." Segine stated. The man watched him carefully.

"My name is Kordimelrichor." Segine nodded slowly then raised his hands above his head, his eyes shining brightly in the barest sliver of moonlight.

"I am Knight Segine Memoria, and this night I send you back to the chaos." The black marks on both arms flowed down and streamed into his hands, forming a sword as black as pitch. The man's thin mouth frowned.

"You have the marks of the Dracolich." Segine lowered his stance.

"I will do what I must." An image of Nysisset filled his mind as he leapt towards his enemy.

* * *

Rielle could hear voices all around her.

"*You don't have to listen to them anymore you know.*" She heard a small, but somehow familiar voice speaking to her. The voices slowly began fading into the background.

"You have had a rough time lately haven't you, miss Rielle." Rielle blinked and slowly opened her eyes, blurry images filling her vision. She saw a movement to her right and felt a gentle hand on her shoulder.

"Miss Rielle?" Rielle recognized Vesth's voice and tried to speak, but her mouth and throat were so dry she only managed to wheeze. She felt the hand carefully lift her head and place something to her lips, pouring cool water into her mouth. She drank for several minutes, taking a few moments in between swallows for breaths. Once she no longer felt dried out, and her stomach began to hurt from drinking, she tried speaking again.

"Is that you Vesth? I can't see anything clearly yet." She still sounded hoarse, but she could at least speak.

"Yes, miss Rielle, I am here." Rielle heard relief in Vesth's voice.

"Where are we?" She let her hand slide along the ground and felt dirt and a few sparse tufts of grass.

"We are on the east face of the Serpent's Tongue Mountains in northern Laytrow." Rielle placed herself on a mental map.

"That would put us a day's journey from the coast?" Rielle saw movement and assumed Vesth had nodded. Vesth turned away and Rielle saw more movement.

"Keliter, could you fill the flask again?" Rielle saw another shape approach.

"Of course." Rielle thought the voice she heard was very familiar.

"Who are you?" She asked. "I feel I have heard your voice before."

"You have." Came the reply. "But that is something you can

worry about at another time. For now, just think of me as a friend." Rielle watched the blurred shape walk away.

"His name is Keliter." She heard Vesth speak and tried to look at him. "I met him shortly after leaving Yal' Tora." Rielle's brow furrowed.

"Yal' Tora? What happened there?" Rielle felt Vesth watching her, and she imagined he probably had a worried look on his face.

"What is the last thing you remember, Miss Rielle?" Rielle tried to recall, but could only remember bits and pieces, along with a few broken images.

"I think I have been walking for a little while, but I don't remember. The last thing I remember fully was heading to my bed chambers after speaking with Lady Quetzalcoatl." Vesth shifted quietly.

"You have been travelling for several days, miss Rielle. You left Terramine the same night. I did not know where you had gone, but I met with Master Solidus who instructed me to meet with the Knight King." Rielle nodded, confused and finding it hard to follow everything being said.

"Take a breath and take a mental step back to collect your thoughts." The familiar quiet voice finally spoke again. Rielle nodded again and breathed deeply, stepping back to look at the information she had already been given.

"Why would Master Solidus send you to speak with the Knight King?" Vesth adjusted his position to be more comfortable.

"Apparently he is the Guardian of the Temple of Water." Rielle blinked a few times, stunned. "Master Solidus knew you were being drawn to the Temple of Water and that the Knight

King could direct me where to find it so that I could meet up with you again." Rielle mulled over the information until she heard Keliter return. Vesth again placed the flask against Rielle's lips and supported her head as she drank.

"So the Knight King is the guardian of the Temple of Water?" She asked after she had finished.

"Indeed." Vesth replied. "Apparently the kings of Laytrow, Hortaal, and Gentry were tasked with protecting the temple's locations." Rielle blinked a few more times, trying to clear her vision.

"So my cousin..." A movement from Vesth told her he had nodded again.

"Yes, the High King is the Guardian of the Temple of Wind."

"That means King Yisu is Guardian of the Temple of Earth. Then who is the Guardian of the Temple of Fire?" Rielle could tell by the way Vesth stiffened that he was frowning deeply.

"Master Solidus said that duty was entrusted to Lord Tiamat. We were instructed to speak with him in his cave once we are done in the Temple of Water." Rielle nodded and carefully sat up. She immediately felt Vesth's hand on her shoulder.

"Do not worry Vesth. My vision has not fully returned, but otherwise I feel well enough." She heard hoof beats coming towards them and the quiet sound of a horse whinnying. "Besides, if Master Delgorin has seen fit to bring my horse along for me, I think it would be best to leave immediately." Rielle heard Keliter walk towards the horse sounds and felt more than saw Vesth turn to watch. There were several seconds of silent communication between the two men and then Vesth turned back.

"It seems you are correct. How did you know Master Delgorin had been here?" Rielle smiled.

"I get the feeling he has been leading those horses around since even before we began our travels. Every time we have purchased a horse, it was likely the same few horses sold to us by Master Delgorin." Rielle felt her heart lighten as Vesth grumbled.

"I wouldn't be surprised to find out the old man had been swindling us repeatedly this whole time." Vesth continued to grumble and Rielle heard Keliter lead a few horses to their small camp.

"I assume that the smaller of the two is yours Miss." Rielle nodded.

"Yes, thank you." Vesth helped Rielle to stand and she felt something slide to the ground. She could hear the quiet whispers again and she became a little disoriented. Vesth hurriedly picked up what had fallen and carefully placed it around her shoulders.

"*No need to listen to them.*" The small voice spoke again. "*Think about your surroundings. Focus on Vesth. The sounds of the horses. Your own curiosity.*" Rielle nodded.

"Thank you. What is this?" Rielle asked, placing one hand on her shoulder. "It is soft, and somehow reminds me of Master Solidus." Vesth carefully led Rielle by the hand.

"Master Solidus gave it to me in Terramine. He said we would need it, and it seems to be helping you recover." Rielle nodded.

"I think it might be. It feels almost familiar. Comforting in a way." Vesth placed her hand on her horse's saddle and put his hand under her right arm for support. Rielle felt another hand, thin but strong, support her left arm. Vesth guided her foot to the stirrup and helped her into the saddle. She felt the one she decided was Keliter hand her the reigns.

"Thank you." She stated, blinking a few times to try and see him more clearly. She could see tan surrounded by what looked almost like sand.

"Might I ask where you are from, Keliter?" Rielle could now make out enough of him to see his head bob up and down in a short nod.

"I am a Telatian Miss. But, as I am sure you are already aware, I am not one of the tainted ones. So you have nothing to fear from me." Rielle nodded slowly, the wheels in her head slowly turning.

"*He is kind of a nice man when he wants to be.*" The voice told her.

"*I have questions for you too.*" Rielle thought outwardly. She heard a chuckle in return.

"*It would be kind of silly if you didn't. But that can wait for another time.*" Rielle nodded.

"As you say, Keliter. As I cannot see you clearly, for now I will trust that Vesth has seen fit to let you travel with us. It is good enough for me." She watched Keliter bow to her.

"Vesth is a formidable warrior. I can think of no better man to stand at your side. I am honored he has trusted me enough to allow me to follow him thus far." Rielle felt at ease from the way he spoke and smiled.

"He is a good friend to me. Perhaps in time you will be too."

"It will be an honor should that day come." This said, Keliter turned to clean up the camp. Rielle held tightly to the reigns and pressed her legs against her horse's sides. She felt it's head shake and it made an affectionate noise. Rielle reached down and patted it's neck with a smile.

"It's nice to see you too." The makeshift camp was cleaned up in a matter of minutes and they began down the mountainside. Rielle could feel Vesth close beside her, keeping her within arms reach should she need a steadying hand.

Keliter took the lead, picking an easy path down the mountain. Rielle could already smell salt in the air, wafting to her on a breeze from the sea.

"*It is such a nice smell.*" Rielle nodded quietly to herself.

"*It is.*" They rode on for several minutes before Rielle chose to speak again. "*So who are you?*" It almost seemed to Rielle that the voice she was speaking to was shuffling around uncomfortably.

"*I am... within the cloak you wear around your shoulders. Well, not in it exactly. I guess it is more accurate to say that the cloak is the anchor that allows me to come back to this world.*" Rielle rode quietly, taking her time to process everything in her still unbalanced thoughts.

"*So you are someone who has passed on to the heaven realms?*"

"*Yep. That's me. I came to help you shut out the voices that call to you from the chaos. The Patriarch is a scar between this world and the void where the chaos dwells. Drawing him from Master Solidus's sealed scabbard allows you to hear those voices. But once you do, you also become scarred and will always be able to hear them. You used The Patriarch to duel Lady Quetzalcoatl, so now you hear the voices calling to you.*"

"Is that why I wandered off?" Rielle asked.

"Hmm?" Vesth asked. Rielle blinked a few times and shook herself.

"Oh, I am sorry Vesth. I didn't realize I had spoken out loud." Vesth nodded.

"I understand. Master Delgorin said you might speak your thoughts out loud once in a while." Rielle nodded.

"Don't worry too much. Gartiel Delgorin explained as much as Vesth could understand. A slip now and then won't worry him any more than he usually does." Rielle went back to her quiet reflection. The ground below them began to level out and Rielle could feel the tall grass of the plains brushing against her boots. Vesth cleared his throat.

"I think we are near Segine's manor house. We could stop there and ask to stay the night. If you wish to." Rielle nodded and tried to look at Vesth more clearly.

"That would be fine. I think a place to take a hot bath would be wonderful right now."

"Then we will try to get there before nightfall. Are you holding up well?" Rielle smiled in Vesth's direction.

"Yes, thank you. My vision is still cloudy, but it is getting clearer. I think a good night's sleep will probably all but clear the fog from my eyes." Vesth nodded again.

"Very well. Please let me know if you need anything before we reach the manor." Rielle smiled again.

"I will, I promise. I just need some time to organize my thoughts." Vesth nodded once again and then tugged on Rielle's reigns to coax her horse into a brisk trot.

"You are doing very well, considering everything you have been through thus far. Consider me impressed." Rielle nodded, bobbing in her saddle.

"I don't think I have the energy to be panicking about small things like gaps in my memory, or what I might have done in

that short period of time." The voice seemed to shuffle around again.

"*You used a great deal of strength getting to this point, that is impressive in it's own right. Believe it or not lesser mages in days past would have died doing what you did in the last few days, and that isn't even considering you also used the Cloak of Sidhe twice during your travels. That is no mean feat.*" Rielle shrugged.

"*You seem a very talkative type.*" An amused laugh sounded in Rielle's mind.

"*Perhaps, but as long as I am talking, it will be that much harder for the voices from the chaos to break through to your conscious thoughts. Besides, I get bored easily and you are the only one who can hear me speak. Though, I guess if Master Solidus was here he might also be able to hear me speaking to you, but I am not quite sure how that works. Neither here nor there I suppose.*" Rielle was beginning to get a peculiar feeling about the voice she was speaking with.

"*I feel I should know your voice somehow.*" The atmosphere of the conversation became instantly sober.

"*Well, You could say that it should be familiar.*" Rielle felt her stomach tighten.

"*I knew you, before you passed to the heaven realms.*" A sad smile filled Rielle's thoughts.

"*I would think so, you practically adopted me. It was fun. Traveling around with you, and mister Vesth and mister Segine, even miss Nysisset was fun to talk to when she wasn't being mean.*" A lump formed in Rielle's throat and tears began to roll down her cheeks.

"Tiasia." She whispered. The sad smile faltered, and Rielle felt the impression of tears.

"Hello, Miss Rielle. I'm so happy to get to see you again."

5

❧

Chapter Five

Vesth sat quietly at the large banquet table. He prodded at his plate with no real appetite for food. Keliter entered the dining hall from a small door set into the far wall. He waved away the servant that offered him a glass of wine and sat down across from Vesth.

"She is sleeping now." Vesth nodded, finally setting aside the uneaten food.

"Did the serving girls say anything about her break down?" Keliter shook his head.

"Miss Rielle didn't speak to any of them except to thank them for their help in getting her cleaned up and into bed. I suspect she came across some painful memories while we were riding and was not able to cope with them properly due to fatigue." Vesth nodded again.

"That does seem a reasonable explanation. Things have not

been easy for us thus far, and there is likely things in her past that I would not know of that could also affect her." Keliter watched Vesth carefully.

"Do you mean to say you do not know of Miss Rielle's past?" Vesth shook his head.

"I have not had occasion to inquire. I know I have heard her name before, during my time as a soldier, but she was an ambassador of some renown in King Yisu's court." Keliter folded his hands together and rested his elbow on the table.

"The High King did his job well then." Vesth eyed Keliter.

"Do you know something of Rielle's past?" Vesth asked, a flash in Keliter's eyes confirming the answer.

"Perhaps." Vesth leaned forward.

"You know something. It shows clearly behind your eyes. What is it that concerns you about Miss Rielle's past?" Keliter shook his head in response.

"That is not for me to say. If you wish to know, you should ask her for yourself. Each person's past is their own burden, and it should only be shared if they wish it to be." Vesth leaned back in his chair again and folded his arms across his chest.

"How do you know of her past then?" Vesth could see an emotionless smile appear on the Telatian's face.

"I know things about many people, especially ones that weigh so heavily on the balance of the world. I also know of your past, and that of the knight Segine Memoria." Vesth frowned.

"What do you know of my past?" Vesth did not like the turn the conversation had taken. Keliter studied Vesth for a few moments and also sat back against his chair.

"If I told you, would you still be able to trust me? Or will my knowledge and my own past break what little trust I have earned from you?" Vesth continued to frown. "I can't say that truthfully without hearing it first. I can say, however, that if you choose to withhold that information from me I will never be able to truly trust you." Keliter nodded once.

"I cannot blame you for that. This world being what it is at this time does not leave room for blind trust." Vesth did not respond, but instead waited for Keliter to continue. Keliter motioned to the servant who was standing dutifully in the corner with the wine. Keliter took the wine and muttered something unintelligible into the servant's ear and the servant nodded and quickly left the room, Keliter keeping his eyes on their back until they were gone.

Keliter poured a glass of wine and offered it to Vesth, who shook his head. Keliter took a sip and set the glass aside.

"Where should I begin?" Vesth watched on quietly.

"How do you know of our past? Mine, Rielle's, and Segine's." Keliter kept careful eye contact with Vesth.

"Our strength, Yours and mine, comes from the same source." He lightly brushed his stomach and Vesth felt his own gut tighten.

"Were you one who was taken by force?" Keliter shook his head.

"A long time ago I was one of the initiated. One who had their gates opened to help control the ones who were taken. But before you get too defensive, I was only with the cult for a very short period of time and I left them more than 15 years ago. I did not appreciate the way they conducted their... business." Keliter sneered, and Vesth could hear just a hint of disdain in his voice, so he chose to let the issue go for the time being.

"So that is why you know so much about the gates." Keliter nodded.

"Indeed. Shortly before the time I left my cult clan, I heard a refugee speaking with our leader about a raid by the Brotherhood. They had destroyed nearly their entire clan, and had made off with an experiment who had not died immediately upon having their first gate pried open. My leader was quiet unhappy about hearing about the loss of such a valuable subject, but it peaked my interest and I went looking for the Brotherhood and the survivor."

"And you found me." Vesth stated bluntly. Keliter nodded again.

"Yes, you were in sorry shape, but I was surprised to find that the Brotherhood had members among it's number that were well enough versed in the gates to close your first gate again for you. I have kept an eye on you since to study your progress. I may not have agreed with the approach the Cult was taking, but it was fascinating to me to finally see someone survive and live a fairly normal life afterwards without being hunted or forced to join one of the branch cults." Vesth scowled.

"I am glad you approve." He said, a little bitterly. Keliter shrugged.

"I merely appreciate your strength and willpower. It is a rare thing to find anymore." Vesth decided it was time to change the subject.

"Is your connection to this cult also how you learned of Miss Rielle's and Segine's past?" Keliter nodded slowly.

"In some part, yes. But theirs is a slightly different kind of tale."

"How so?" A grin slowly crept onto Keliter's face, and Vesth's hands gripped tightly onto his folded arms.

"Let us just say," Keliter said, lifting his wine glass up to his lips. "That our stories, yours and mine, are commonplace and dull compared to theirs."

* * *

Rielle was sitting in a large and very soft armchair, watching a warm fire burn in a beautiful stone fireplace. Tiasia came from somewhere behind her and placed a tray with cups and a teapot onto the small table beside her.

"How do you like my room?" Tiasia asked, pouring Rielle a cup of tea. Rielle took the cup Tiasia handed her and looked around the room. It was very simple, the fireplace being the only real feature in the room other than a small potted plant in one corner and a door on each end of the room.

"It is very nice." Rielle smiled as Tiasia giggled and sat down in a chair across from her.

"The Matriarch let me make it when she told me I would be traveling with you again." Rielle sipped at her tea, which tasted sweet and warmed her whole body.

"You made it yourself?" Tiasia nodded excitedly, holding up her two hands and a small flower appeared between them.

"Yep, I can do magic now too Miss Rielle. Though, The Matriarch asked me to be careful if I used it a bunch because I have to draw the elements directly from the chaos." Rielle could not help but smile at the little girl who was so excited, even though she could still feel the sadness trying to creep in. Tiasia smiled softly back, letting the flower disappear.

"You don't have to be sad any more Miss Rielle. I had to go

to the heaven realm so that they could teach me how to help protect you." Rielle's smile saddened slightly.

"I promised to protect you, and I failed." Tiasia stood and walked quietly to Rielle, wiping away a tear at the corner of her eye, then wrapped her arms around her neck and hugged her tightly.

"You did protect me. You saved me from the angry eyes of my village. You protected me from the darkness that had formed in my heart from loneliness. You did more for me in the short time we were together than anyone else in my life had ever even considered. And even if you had known what was going to happen to me, Master Solidus would not have allowed you to stop it. I needed to go to the heaven realm so I could do the same for you as you had for me." Rielle felt another tear roll down her cheek and placed one hand on Tiasia's back.

"Thank you. You are far more forgiving than I deserve." Tiasia stepped back and shook her head.

"Not at all, Miss Rielle. Your life when you were my age was just as hard, maybe even harder." Rielle blinked in surprise.

"How..."

"I told her, Rielle." Rielle looked over her shoulder and watched Solidus enter through one of the doors and close it behind him. Tiasia got really excited and rushed to him, hugging him around his waist.

"Master Solidus! You came to see me." Solidus smiled and patted her on the head.

"Indeed, little one. I had to come and see your home, it is lovely so far." Tiasia took a step back and nodded, blushing a little.

"Thank you. It isn't done yet though." Solidus nodded

heading over and sitting down in the vacant chair, Tiasia closely in tow.

"Working with the chaos directly is very difficult, what you have managed in such a short time is impressive. I am sure it will be a wondrous place when you finish." Tiasia nodded with a big smile, and then got fidgety.

"I met her." Solidus smiled widely, his silver eyes shimmering.

"And?"

"She is really pretty. And she was super nice and taught me lots of things. And she showed me how to speak with the Matriarch and the Patriarch and told me lots of stories about you when you were young." Solidus laughed.

"I am sure she did." Solidus looked past the little girl and smiled at Rielle. "And how have you been holding up, young one? I imagine things have been tough since last we spoke." Rielle shook her head.

"No harder than I expected it to be, though I didn't really expect to meet Lady Quetzalcoatl after I spoke with Lady Sidhe." Tiasia backed up a little and stood next to Solidus.

"Lady Sidhe is kind of scary." Solidus smiled and placed his hand on her head again.

"She is just passionate, she tends to forget that it can get a little overwhelming at times." Rielle was swimming with questions and Solidus gave her a knowing look.

"You can ask whatever you want." Rielle blushed and Tiasia giggled.

"How are you here Master Solidus?" Solidus smiled.

"You think you are dreaming?" Rielle hesitated for a moment, but then she nodded slowly.

"This is actually a place between the world you live in and the Heaven Realm. While your body is resting your spirit traveled here to get rest as well." Rielle looked at her hand.

"My spirit?" Solidus nodded.

"Indeed. If you try you will notice that you cannot get up from your chair. It is because you are still anchored to the world and that chair is the only place you can visit outside of the world." Rielle tried, but her legs would not respond and she could only manage to lean forward.

"Are you here in spirit too then?" Solidus nodded.

"Back in your body you would see me as the shimmering outline you have seen before, but here, in the void, spirits are much more solid." Rielle nodded.

"Then why did you come here? Other than to see Tiasia of course." She quickly corrected herself when Tiasia frowned.

"I came for two reasons." Solidus answered. "First was to check the tethers that bind our world to the Heaven Realm. They can also effect the balance, so it is my responsibility. However I can only travel half way, as I am forbidden from traveling to the Heaven Realm until my charge is through." Tiasia pouted.

"It is really sad. You can't even go to see her. It's not fair." Solidus rubbed the little girl's head, messing up her hair.

"It's not so bad. I can still speak with her if I wish, and I am doing what I am because of her. I have waited this long, waiting a little longer won't be too much trouble." Curiosity overcame Rielle.

"Who are you talking about?" Tiasia opened her mouth excitedly.

"Lady mmmph..." Solidus conjured a large bread roll from

nothing and stuffed it into Tiasia's mouth. Tiasia mumbled, trying to talk around it, but ended up just chewing dejectedly.

"My Deity. It was she who tasked me with protecting the balance, And I will continue to do so until my task is done and I am allowed to return to the Heaven Realm." Solidus smiled back at Tiasia.

"Sorry little one, but remember, Rielle is still of the World and my Lady's name must remain unspoken to living ears until the world is in balance." Tiasia nodded, mumbling what Rielle assumed was 'ok' around her roll.

"And what was your second reason for coming?" Rielle asked, and Solidus once again turned back to her.

"To see you, of course. I wanted to make sure you are well, the chaos is a difficult thing to listen to, especially for those who have not learned the arts necessary to protect themselves from it." Rielle nodded.

"I understand. I don't really remember anything after I met Lady Quetzalcoatl." Solidus nodded.

"Your mind was unable to comprehend the voices you heard, so it shut down and you began acting on instinct alone. Fortunately your instincts drove you to find the Temple of Water." Rielle tried to think back, but could not.

"Is that why you sent Vesth to find his own way to the Temple of Water?" Solidus nodded.

"Indeed. He would not likely have caught up to you alone, so I sent him ahead so that he would end up on the path you would most likely travel. Of course, on the small chance that you went a different way, I sent Delgorin to keep an eye on him." Rielle nodded, settling back into her own thoughts and forming questions to ask.

"Since you are here, Master Solidus, do you know of a man named Keliter?" Solidus smiled and Tiasia giggled.

"He reminds me of mister Vesth." Tiasia stated then grumbled and tried to push down her hair as Solidus messed it up again.

"Whether you trust him or not is up to you." He said, finally giving up his attack on the little girl's hair and turning his head back to Rielle. "But he can be a valuable ally to you. He has knowledge of many things and can also open the gates the same way Vesth can." Rielle blinked in surprise.

"Where have I met him before? I think I know him, but I feel I would remember someone like that more readily." Solidus smiled.

"You will remember when you see him. Just try to remain objective and weigh all options before making a judgment." Rielle frowned, not liking the way Solidus had phrased his words. Then she recalled what Tiasia had said before.

"How does Tiasia know of my past?" Solidus smiled, though sadly.

"I told her, of course. Your mind has come into contact with the chaos, and as such shadows of your past will now reside there. Should Borsa, his demon, or any of his followers find those shadows they will try to use them against you. Even after all these years it is still a sore memory for you, so it was best that Tiasia knew before it came up so she can prepare herself, with the Matriarch's help, to help you through the trial, should it arise." Rielle nodded, seeing the reason behind the action.

"I suppose I need not ask how you knew." She responded. Solidus chuckled.

"I may be a hermit, but I haven't spent the last thousand

years solely in the mountains." Solidus leaned back in his chair, waving his hand through the air and creating a silver chalice, filled with liquid. It reminded Rielle of the way the Deity of Evil had acted when they first met him.

"Even back then you weighed heavily on the Balance. During the... events, the balance in Terramine was disturbed, mainly around you. I watched as events unfolded and, after making sure everything had righted itself and after having a few words with your uncle, returned to the Mercury mountains." Rielle sat her teacup on the table beside her.

"You spoke with my uncle?" Solidus nodded.

"Your cousin Morien had taken to protecting you even though the court thought differently. Since your Uncle was High King at the time I thought it wise to give him council, though I did so indirectly as he would not have known who I was." Rielle thought quietly for a few moments, smiling at Tiasia as she refilled her cup with tea.

"So you convinced my Uncle to pass the ruling he did?" Solidus smiled again, but shook his head.

"No. In fact, even to my surprise, he chose to leave the decision to his young son, your cousin. It was Morien's first official declaration as High Prince, and he challenged any who opposed the decision to a duel. Of course, even then your cousin was quiet skilled with a sword and none in the court dared to face him openly." Rielle smiled, picturing her cousins face.

"He has always treated me like a little sister. He is far too kind to me." Tiasia grinned.

"I like him. I think a ruler should always be kind. You can't be a good ruler if your people are afraid of you and try to run away. It doesn't make any sense."

"And yet there are those who choose to rule through fear. Because it is the easier path." Solidus noted. "But fear is not in the balance of the world. Fear pulls at the world, and eventually the world will pull back. Turning fear into anger, and anger into hatred. Hatred creates bravery and strength from nothing and eventually what was feared becomes hunted. A leader who rules through fear will eventually be brought down by it, no matter how hard they struggle against it." Rielle nodded her agreement, thinking of Borsa, a little fire growing in her chest.

"But be careful not to let hatred turn your heart either. Hatred also brings imbalance and causes hearts and minds to break, and reason to die. Righteous anger is one thing, But blind hatred is a sin of it's own." Rielle felt as if Solidus could see right through her and swallowed, carefully extinguishing her angry flame. Solidus smiled warmly and then looked towards the ceiling.

"Ah, things have shifted once again. It is time for me to go." He stood from his chair and Tiasia rushed to his side.

"Do you have to go?" She asked, pouting at him. He tousled her hair again.

"Of course, little one. We all have things to do, and Rielle must wake from her rest soon." Tiasia frowned.

"Oh, yeah. I almost forgot." Solidus smiled.

"Do not worry, you are almost to the Temple of Water. Great Titan Perion is already waiting for you there. You wouldn't want to keep him waiting would you?" Tiasia shook her head.

"No, I think he would probably get lonely." Solidus laughed.

"I'm sure he would." He turned back to Rielle. "Be careful in the Temple. There are still remnants there of the old

Guardian. Once you are through there, you should travel to the entrance of Tiamat's cave. Someone will be waiting there to speak with you." Rielle nodded.

"Thank you Master Solidus." Soldius patted her hand as he walked past.

"Do not worry, all will be well." A strange glint in his silver eyes gave Rielle an uncomfortable feeling and she nodded silently as he left. Once he was gone Tiasia sighed.

"I guess it is back to work for now." She said, quiet for a moment, then turning and almost skipping to Rielle's side.

"Will you come back to see me again sometime?" Rielle nodded.

"Of course I will." She smiled, Tiasia's excited expression washing away any worries she felt. Then Tiasia sat on the arm of Rielle's chair and wrapped her arms around her again.

"Then I will try to make my room even better for you next time." Rielle nodded and reached up, smoothing the little girl's messy hair.

"I am sure it will be wonderful." She said, suddenly feeling very sleepy. Tiasia rested her head against Rielle's.

"Remember that we are all with you. You don't have to journey alone. You can lean on all of us when you need rest. Mister Vesth will stand beside you to the end, and you will be reunited with mister Segine and miss Nysisset some day." Rielle felt her eyes fluttering shut.

"I will try to remember."

"Yes, and when you wake continue onward." Rielle's eyes closed and she felt herself drifting away.

"Rest well, Miss Rielle. And be strong." The words trailed to Rielle, barely reaching her ears as she floated through darkness. She drifted silently for what seemed like hours, then she felt warmth and saw a shimmer of light. She felt herself enter the presence of something the likes of which she had never felt before.

"Hear my voice, Mortal whose fate is tied to the balance." The voice was deep, and powerful. Rielle could feel each word resonating throughout her entire body.

"Hear my Voice. It is time to remember the Lessons taught. To relearn the Strength needed to heal the wounds of the chaos, and right the wrongs of the past." The light grew brighter and Rielle squeezed her eyes tightly shut, trying to block it out.

"Gain the Power you need and become a Beacon of hope to those who have none." Thousands of images flooded Rielle's mind. Flashes of people with blurred faces, individually directing her to learn and remember. Motions she saw herself perform, for battle, for magic, and for grace flashing through her mind's eye faster than she could process them.

"Wake and Begin the Battle!" Rielle jerked awake, sitting upright in her bed with a gasp. She looked around the unfamiliar room for several seconds before she remembered where she was.

The door to her right opened and a young servant girl rushed in.

"Are you alright miss?" She seemed a little worried. Rielle nodded and rubbed her eyes for a moment to clear the sleep from them. She blinked a few times and looked back over to the servant girl, glad that her vision had finally cleared.

"Yes, thank you. Do you know the time of day?" The girl nodded.

"Indeed miss, it is just before noon. Lunch is being served

as we speak." Rielle nodded and rolled her shoulders, feeling a little achy, but otherwise well enough.

"Could you bring me my fresh clothes then? I am feeling a bit hungry and would like to join the household for the noon meal if I may." The girl bowed hurriedly.

"Of course miss. I will speak with my mistress and arrange for it immediately." Rielle nodded and smiled kindly.

"Thank you." The girl bowed again and rushed out. It was only a few minutes before several more servant girls entered her room and helped her to stand and dress. They lead her out of her door into a wide, modestly decorated hall where Rielle, unsurprisingly, found Vesth waiting for her.

"Are you feeling well this morning?" He asked her. She nodded politely.

"I am, thank you Vesth. I hope I did not cause you to worry overmuch." Vesth nodded, though she saw a slight smile tug at the corner of his lips.

"A bit formal today?" Rielle almost laughed, realizing she had forgotten she was speaking in her courtly manner.

"Oh, I am sorry. I forgot myself. I hope you didn't stand in the hallway waiting for me all night." Vesth shook his head.

"Keliter was the voice of reason and suggested I get at least a few hours of sleep before I did." Rielle looked up and down the hall.

"Which reminds me, where is he? Is he eating right now?" Vesth nodded.

"He was, but he said he wished to speak with you privately once you have eaten so he took some food and went to wait in Segine's private study." Rielle nodded, thinking quietly before she remembered the servant girls grouped up behind her.

"Oh, thank you ladies for helping me dress. I think this soldier here can lead me to the dining hall. You may return to your other duties." The girls all giggled at being called ladies, but curtsied and left down the hall in a small group.

Vesth offered his arm and, still not sure how steady she felt, Rielle accepted it and they turned down a smaller hall and through a doorway before entering the main dining hall. Rielle sat down at the table, a few old knights and ladies all nodding to her politely.

"Did you sleep well?" Vesth asked her after she had a few bites to eat.

"I think so. I dreamed and felt a little disconnected from myself, so I don't know for sure." Vesth nodded and waited quietly while she ate. Rielle could tell there was something he wanted to ask, but he remained quiet and let her finish eating. Once she finished she sat back against her chair and waited for him to speak. He remained silent for a few moments more before relenting.

"Would you mind too much if I asked what caused you to cry yesterday?" Rielle felt a slight guilty twinge in her stomach.

"You don't have to tell me if you don't want to." Vesth added. Rielle nodded.

"It's ok. I just remembered some things suddenly and I wasn't prepared emotionally for it. I am sorry if I worried you." Vesth shook his head.

"Don't be sorry, you were exhausted. Anyone in that position might have broken down from painful memories. Were they recent memories? Or ones long past?" Again, Rielle got the feeling that there was an unasked question lurking somewhere behind Vesth's eyes. She smiled at him.

"I was thinking of Tiasia." She saw a pained expression cross his features for barely an instant.

"I see." He said. He almost seemed relieved. Rielle watched him closely until he spoke again.

"I will admit, I realized that I know very little about your past before we met, other than you were an ambassador. I was a little worried that you might be reliving painful memories which I would not be able to understand." Rielle smiled, suddenly understanding.

"I see. There are perhaps a few of those left that I have buried away inside me. I haven't thought about them in years though." Vesth nodded.

"You know, It might not be such a bad idea to tell mister Vesth sometime. A burden is always easier to carry when others can help you carry it." Rielle struggled internally, but didn't really like the idea.

"Its ok if you don't want to. But if you ever feel like you need to vent, I think mister Vesth is probably the best person you could talk to. And I don't think your cousin the High King would mind if you did. Vesth wouldn't tell anyone else." Rielle clenched her jaw a little, trying not to make any decisions rashly.

"Perhaps one day I may. But not right now." Rielle felt Tiasia shrug but didn't hear any more.

"Will you go meet with Keliter now?" Vesth asked. Rielle shook herself a little to snap herself back to the present.

"I guess I should. I did wish to ask him some questions." Vesth nodded, though he didn't seem very happy.

"What's wrong?" Rielle asked him. He shrugged, but looked around to see if anyone was close enough to hear him.

"I spoke with him last night and he told me some things

which has brought my trust of him into question. Though I know I am judging him on past experiences instead of the things he has done to help us in the present. I was hoping you would be able to think more objectively and make a more fair decision." Rielle frowned.

"What did he tell you?" Vesth shuffled a little uncomfortably.

"He knows a lot about our pasts. Mine, yours and Segine's. He said he would not speak of your past without permission, but what he told me of my own leads me to believe he is telling the truth." Rielle felt an uncomfortable knot in her stomach beginning to form.

"How did he learn about our past's?" Vesth shrugged.

"I do not know the whole story. He told me why he knows about me, but I think it is different for you and Segine. He did not seem too keen on telling me." Rielle nodded, resisting the urge to bite her nails as she thought. She felt Tiasia place a small hand on her shoulder.

"*I don't think it is as bad as it sounds.*" Rielle nodded again, trying to push the worst case scenarios out of her mind.

"Very well then. Take me to see Keliter. I will ask him myself and see how he answers." Vesth stood with a nod and helped her stand. They left the dining hall and made their slow way up a flight of spiral stairs and down another hall to a set of double doors. A page stood between the two doors.

"Master Keliter asked that I only allow Lady Rielle to enter the study." He said nervously, looking up at Vesth's scowling face. Rielle patted Vesth's arm for reassurance and nodded to the page, who opened the door for her. Rielle stepped through the door, seeing Vesth lean against the opposite wall, loosening his sword in it's scabbard before the door fully closed.

The room was simple. A desk sat at the back of the room, covering most of the back wall. Paintings of numerous knights lined the walls to either side ending with three on the wall above the desk. One of the paintings was obviously Segine, and Rielle guessed that it was likely that the other two were his father and Grandfather. The chair behind the desk was large and made of heavy oak, with dark red velvet cushions on the back and arms. In the chair sat a slim figure in a sand colored cloak with his hood drawn up to cover his face, nearly dwarfed by the large chair he sat in.

"Please come in miss Rielle. I hope you don't mind me keeping my face covered for the time being. I wish us to speak for a little while before I uncovered it. I would like a chance to present my case, so to speak, before I am judged." Rielle nodded slowly and made her way to a chair that had been set in front of the desk.

"If you are willing to remove your hood before we are done here, then I will accept that for now." Keliter nodded.

"Thank you. Before we get started I would like you to look on the desk in front of you. I have disarmed myself and left my weapon there for you to inspect." Rielle looked down to see a long knife on the end of the desk. She lifted it carefully and pulled it part way from it's scabbard. She was shocked to see a rearing dragon looking back at her.

"You are a Dragon Blade?" Keliter nodded.

"Yes. Since The High Priest of Telatia is not in good standing with the Temple of Fire and Earth I had to travel to Gentry to be tested in the court there. King Yisu's advisers tested me and found me worthy of receiving my own blade. I was even allowed to meet with Taeldora Marina who allowed me to design my own weapon. Though at the time, I did not know she was one of the Mages of Alenon." Rielle nodded. And placed the knife back on the table.

"But you know now." Keliter nodded again.

"Indeed. I heard rumors shortly after I left Tyr' Anon that the smith at the Temple of Fire and Earth had lived far longer than any normal person. When I investigated she had already left the temple with a party who's description matched yours. Eventually I found a sailor, drunk at a tavern, who claimed he had sailed to the ends of the world and back taking a group of the same description to the Temple Island of Alenon. It was not hard to guess at that point who she was." Rielle watched Keliter, searching him for any body language that would tell her anything, but he was being careful to keep a very neutral pose.

"So when did you leave Tyr' Anon?" She asked.

"Four days before the Blood Moon Cycle."

"And how did you get outside of Telatia?" Keliter sat back slightly in his chair and Rielle could tell he was smiling.

"With Master Solidus having destroyed the Great Gates I was forced to take more treacherous paths." Rielle did her best to keep a neutral expression, though she very much wanted to frown.

"And what path was that? We took one path through the mountains after the Blood Moon to enter Telatia, but it is not a path a normal mortal can tread." Keliter nodded.

"I am aware that you entered Telatia through Tiamat's cave, but that is not the only way out of Telatia. There are a few paths, some that cross over the mountains, and a few that even pass beneath. Though they are very dangerous and most who cross them die doing so. I know that there were several Nibilus who tried to cross behind me but, none of them made it to the other side." Rielle thought quietly, processing the information.

"*Do you know anything about paths across the Serpents Tongue mountains.*" She asked internally. She felt Tiasia nod.

"*There are two dangerous paths that go over the tops, but they are considered virtually impassable.*" Rielle could imagine the little girl sprawled out on the floor of her small room with a large map, pointing out locations as she spoke.

"*There is also one path left that travels under the mountains, but it passes through one of the old fairy grotto's, so getting through unscathed would be very difficult. The other paths still available have either been destroyed over the years, or require powerful spells to open, like the portal at Master Solidus's house that we used to go to Alenon when Mister Segine was hurt.*" Rielle waited patiently for Tiasia to finish before she asked her next question.

"Vesth told me you helped him find me. How were you able to do so?" Keliter folded his hands together and rested his elbows on the arms of the chair.

"To a small extent I am able to sense the threads of balance in the world and how they pull on each other. Since you are tied to the balance it is easier to follow where you are going since you pull at the threads around you. Your companions are much the same way." Rielle inspected the man before her.

"So you are like master Solidus then?" Keliter laughed, little more than an amused chuckle.

"I am like Master Solidus in the same way a Sapling is like the entire Moon Witch Forest. I am made of much the same thing, yet What master Solidus can see and do is so much more vast than I, that there can really be no true comparison.

But I can see some things. I could see threads coming undone around the High Priest and it grew worse and worse until the time before the Blood Moon Cycle when I decided it was no longer safe to stay within the city. The same ability allowed me to cross the mountains and find sure enough footing to get across alive." Rielle nodded. So far she felt no reason to believe he was lying to her.

"Why did you decide to help us?" Keliter scratched his barely visible chin.

"I could see the balance around you was mending, growing stronger, rather than falling apart. And you move with purpose. You have decided a fate for yourself and you work toward it with all your strength. It is something I have not seen before. I have watched the High Priest, who also moves with purpose, but his purpose seems to be but a means to an end. For you, it feels more like each thing you do matters just as much as your end goal. And those who travel with you, you treat with as much importance as your task at hand." Rielle nodded.

"That is because they are. What point is there in protecting this world, restoring balance to everything, If I must sacrifice those I care about to do it? I do not care how much harder it may be, I will fight to keep them safe, no matter the cost. My friends, my loved ones, they are the reason I continue to fight. They give me strength and hold me up when nothing else can." Keliter nodded slowly.

"I see. So you have many reasons for following the path you do. You do not let one reason or another pull you off course. You allow everything and everyone around you to strengthen you, acting as a part of the world, and not separate from it."

"*That is what it means to be within the balance.*" Tiasia

seemed more calm than she normally was. "*Allowing the flow of the world to carry you and acting within that flow without ever letting it pull you away from your chosen course. Never giving up, and never changing who you are or your ideals while still helping the rest of the world to achieve their ideals without forcing them to change. That is how one works with, and finds true strength, within the balance.*"

"What goal do you work for?" Rielle asked. Keliter continued to gaze at his clasped hands.

"I think for now, my only purpose is to find a purpose. Until now I have allowed those around me to carry me with their ideals. But I have never felt entirely at ease in my station. I always feel as if there is something more, something I am missing. Perhaps it is because I allowed the ideals of another to guide me, rather than searching for my own." Keliter looked up from his hands and looked at Rielle.

"What I do know, is that if I sit back and allow the world to fall to ruin, I will never find that purpose." Keliter reached up and took hold of his hood.

"Please, Lady Rielle," He pulled back his hood and Rielle pressed her hand over her mouth to avoid gasping. "Allow me to join you in stopping Borsa Kera Moradon from unraveling this world."

6

Chapter Six

Vesth watched Rielle carefully as they rode. She had not taken her eyes off of Keliter since the moment they had left Segine's manor, and Vesth did not like the expression on her face.

When she had left the study she was very unhappy, but when he asked her why, she told him that everything was fine and that they needed to move on. Keliter led the way, keeping a respectful distance from them, and riding at a steady pace.

They stopped before dark and made a camp, lighting two camp fires to light up the area. Vesth and Keliter took turns on watch, keeping the fires going and keeping an eye out for Nibilus. Just before the light of dawn began to outline the mountains, Keliter joined Vesth.

"Can you hear them?" Keliter asked, his voice ominously quiet. Vesth nodded.

"They are circling, trying to hide their footsteps in the dark." Keliter threw a few more logs on to each fire and fanned the flames.

"If they are doing their best to stay quiet, then there has to be something directing them." Vesth nodded.

"Every time I have encountered the Nibilus they have acted almost like wild dogs. Barking and yapping." Keliter scanned the darkness beyond the firelight.

"That is how they communicate. But if they are moving silently, then something else is directing them so they have no need of communication." Vesth also scanned the darkness, sparing a glance at Keliter.

"A Basilisk?" Keliter shrugged, though he threw another log on the nearest fire.

"Or a demon. Hopefully whatever it is will not decide to act before first light."

"That is a bit wishful." Both men turned to see Rielle, sitting quietly on her bed roll, staring into the darkness.

"They are more likely to act as dawn draws closer. Hoping to act before they must flee the sun's light." Keliter examined the slowly growing outline above the mountains and grabbed a burning log from one of the fires, throwing it on the remaining unburned wood, quickly creating a third fire.

"Hopefully whoever is in charge will realize we are onto them and not wish to risk their numbers in open combat." Rielle continued to stare in one direction.

"He is already aware." Vesth scowled and drew his sword, the blade flashing in the fire light. They heard a skitter in the distance, something trying to escape the flash. Rielle did not react.

"He does not care. He does not fear us." She stood and turned towards the darkness. Vesth took a step to follow, But Rielle held up her hand.

"Stay here." Vesth would have spoken, but Keliter placed a hand on his shoulder, shaking his head and motioning at Rielle. Vesth turned back and saw that Rielle's eyes were cold as ice and hard as steel. He struggled inwardly for a moment, but eventually relented. Once he had, Rielle turned her hand palm up and held it out.

"Your sword." Vesth reversed his grip and placed the sword in her hand. She nodded once and then walked out into the darkness. Vesth grumbled and picked up a solid branch, lighting one end on fire and then wielding it like a sword. Vesth and Keliter stood back to back between the three fires, weapons raised, ready to defend themselves.

Vesth felt the air around him grow cold and heard a wet hiss and a thud as something hit the ground nearby. They heard a growl from the other end of the camp, followed almost immediately by another hiss and thud. The sounds repeated several more times and then everything around them was silent, save for the occasional pop from the fires.

After several minutes Keliter nudged Vesth, motioning away from the fires with his head. Vesth looked and found himself staring directly into two large yellow eyes. They were at the far edge of the light, only barely visible, and Vesth could barely make out a large, wolf-like muzzle below them.

"So that is a Basilisk." Keliter nodded.

"Indeed." The Basilisk dared another step forward. It's huge frame, covered in a thick black mane, was almost visible in the dim light.

"You play a dangerous game." Vesth nearly jumped when Rielle's voice sounded beside them. She walked silently past him, his sword hanging comfortably in her hand, dripping with blood that hissed and sizzled as it came into the light of the fires.

"Do you think you are strong enough to fight us in the light?" Vesth gripped his branch tightly, hearing it creak, as the Basilisk's eyes flashed intelligently. It grinned, it's mouth full of sharpened teeth, and spoke.

"You think you are strong enough to do battle with me as you are?" It's voice was coarse and dry, and rumbled deep in it's throat.

"No mortal can oppose me. The ages have weakened you, and strengthened me." Rielle raised Vesth's sword above her head with both hands, in a stance that Vesth had never seen before. Rielle's eyes grew bright and her voice seemed to echo from all around them.

"I was taught by The Balance Mage, Grandmaster Pravin Solidus. My magic was inherited from my bloodline, the bloodline of Hortaal Lyvinius. I carry the Cloak of Soaring Zephyr Sidhe, And the blessing of Dragon Guardian Quetzalcoatl. My strength is that of all the ages past, my power that of the World itself. My Strength is far more ancient than your own, and it is no less overwhelming for the ages it has endured." The air around them grew heavy and both Vesth and Keliter dug their heels into the ground and braced themselves.

"Do you think your borrowed titles will frighten me?" The Basilisk responded, it's long claws raking the ground. Rielle shook her head.

"I do not tell you this to try and frighten you. I speak the truth so that the one I see, watching from behind your eyes, will hear. Nothing you send after me will stay me from my course. Your servants will fall before me and others until only you remain. Then it will be your turn to face me, and you will be thrust back into the chaos and balance will be restored." The Basilisk's grin grew broad and evil, it's eyes turning a burning red and when it spoke, it spoke in a low raspy voice.

"We Shall See." Rielle shouted wordlessly, her entire body cloaked in mist and Vesth's sword burst into flames. She moved in a streak of light, encircling the Basilisk before striking it across the head. The plains erupted in an explosion of flames that roared twenty feet into the sky. Vesth drove his branch into the ground as the angry wind tore at him. He felt Keliter open his gates and use the energy to drive the wind away from him.

Rielle stood among the flames, spinning Vesth's sword in graceful arcs, throwing disks of flame to wash over the howling Basilisk. With one final shout, The blade of Vesth's sword blazed into brilliant golden light and Rielle drove it deep into the Basilisk's skull.

With a final howl the Basilisk's body dissolved into black ash that was carried away by the roaring flames. The flames continued to blaze for several more moments before quickly dying down into nothing, leaving no sign that anything had been there just moments before.

Rielle turned, flicking the sword blade, and dismissing the mist around her. She passed the blade to Vesth and returned to her bed roll.

"I must rest before the sun rises. Wake me when we are ready to leave." She laid down and covered herself, quickly becoming still and quiet. Vesth wiped his blade, though it had no real need to be cleaned, and returned it to it's scabbard.

"Something has changed about her." Vesth stated. Keliter breathed deeply, closing his gates Vesth assumed.

"Indeed. She seems to have gained something she did not have before." Vesth nodded.

"She did not seem to have enough skill to handle fire on that scale before now." Vesth glanced back over his shoulder at the ground behind them.

"And yet," Keliter stated, following his eyes. "She managed to destroy a Basilisk, an ancient being of undetermined strength, and did so without so much as scorching the ground around it." Vesth nodded.

"I do not like how quickly things are beginning to progress." Keliter nodded, his face sober.

"I almost feel like we are being pushed towards something, and our strength to handle what we encounter seems to grow as we move onward." Vesth turned back to the camp, pulling apart and stamping out their third fire.

"I guess we should get what rest we can before the sun rises." Keliter nodded again.

"Indeed. You sleep and I will keep watch. I can lead us to where the Temple of Water is located, but you are likely the only one who can find the entrance." Vesth nodded and returned to his bed roll, laying down and quickly falling asleep.

Vesth's dreams were vague shadows that he could not clearly see or understand. He woke, just as light was beginning to peek over the mountains. The three fires were no more than smoldering cinders, and Keliter was already stamping them out and burying them. Vesth could see several smoldering ash piles littering the area around the camp.

"The bodies of the slain Nibilus." Keliter stated, noticing Vesth's curious glance. "They began to burn as soon as the light of dawn began to show over the mountains. The ash will likely burn away when they are hit by sunlight directly." Vesth nodded, sparing the piles one more glance before standing and clearing away his own things. He carefully woke Rielle and helped her to stand.

"Are you well?" Vesth quickly tied her bedroll and packed it on her horse.

"I will be fine. Last night is a bit of a blur to me still, but I feel rested and I should be ready by the time we reach the temple." Vesth nodded and then motioned to Keliter. Keliter signaled that they were ready to leave and Vesth offered his hand and helped Rielle up into her saddle.

They left at a steady trot, Keliter leading the way several paces ahead. By mid morning they reached a small hill that overlooked the coast. The beach was choked with large smooth boulders that had been exposed as the sand was washed away by centuries of waves. Keliter pointed at the beach.

"Down there is where you will find the Temple of Water. I do not know where the entrance is, But I assume The Knight King explained to you how to find it." He glanced over at Vesth, who nodded.

"I was given instructions on how to find it." Keliter nodded, and then dismounted. Vesth looked at him questioningly. Keliter shrugged at the unspoken question.

"Even from here I can sense the Deity of Water waiting for you. I hail from Telatia, the land of fire, and I have been in the presence of Borsa. I do not think I will be welcome in the Temple. I will keep watch here." Vesth turned to look at Rielle who nodded.

"That may be a wise descision. As I understand, The Deity of Water can be overzealous at times." Keliter nodded in return.

"Then I will make a small camp here and await your return." Rielle nodded once more and then looked at Vesth.

"We should move quickly. I can already sense something in the Temple beginning to stir. Lead the way Vesth." Vesth turned back and urged his horse down the hill and out onto the rocky shore, Rielle close behind. They traveled along the beach for several minutes, Vesth scanning the area carefully, until they came to a sand bar that extended a short way out into ocean water. Vesth dismounted, handing his reigns to Rielle, and climbed over a few rocks to get a better look. He returned and gave Rielle a nod.

"This is the right place." She returned his nod and he helped her down from her horse, tying his reigns to her saddle once she was down. They climbed over the rocks and continued down the sand bar, being careful not to slip on the smooth wet stones that littered it.

At the other end stood a large pile of boulders that extended from the sand, preventing the ocean waves from washing over the beach. Vesth approached the boulders and inspected them, immediately finding what looked to be scratch marks on their surface.

"This is it." Rielle joined him and placed one hand against the surface of the boulder.

"I can sense great power here." She said, placing her other hand against the boulder and looking around. "But how do we get inside the Temple?" Vesth sighed and Rielle gave him a questioning look. Vesth shook his head and also placed his hands against the boulder and cleared his throat.

"Great Titan Perion, Hear our cries and allow our unworthy eyes to behold the magnificence of your home. And allow us to stand in your Glorious presence."

* * *

Vesth called out as if the boulder they were touching would answer them. Rielle glanced at Vesth out of the corner of her eye, doing her best not to laugh, though a smile touched her lips. Vesth grumbled.

"That is what the Knight King told me to say when I got here." Rielle drew breath to speak when the ground around them began to shake. To her surprise, the boulder in front of them rose further from the sand and then the center seemed to melt away to reveal a staircase downward. Rielle blinked several times in surprise. Vesth straightened his back and coughed once.

"I suppose that means the Knight King gave me the correct instructions." Rielle glanced at him and then back down into the darkness that swallowed the staircase.

"*Great Titan Perion likes to be flattered.*" Tiasia said with a giggle. "*He likes to act tough and powerful, but I think he is really nice.*" Rielle nodded. She could smell a damp, musty scent rising from the staircase now.

"Are you ready?" Vesth asked her. She nodded very slowly.

"I think so. But Master Solidus said to be careful, there may be remnants of the old guardian down there..." Her voice trailed off, a few whispers entering her thoughts.

"*These whispers are ok to listen to.*" Tiasia told her. "*They come from The Patriarch. He is trying to help you.*" Rielle tried to block out everything she could from around her and listen. Shadowy images flitted across her mind, as if she was trying to recall something she had seen before, but could not quite remember. She got the impression of glittering scales and crystal blue water that quickly turned dark and noxious. She felt as if she were drowning and quickly opened her eyes and forced herself to breath. Vesth gave her a worried look.

"Are you alright?" Rielle nodded again.

"Yes, thank you Vesth. I felt like I might have known what is down there for a moment." She motioned towards the stairs. "Like something on the tip of my tongue that I can't quite remember." Vesth nodded.

"I will lead the way." He said, loosing his sword from it's scabbard. "Please stay close behind." Rielle smiled and nodded.

"I will provide us with light." She said, holding out her hand and creating a small orb of soft golden light. Vesth nodded once more before turning and picking his careful way down the stairs. Rielle walked along behind him, trying to hold her light high enough for Vesth to see through the darkness below them.

They made their way down for several minutes, trying not to slip on the wet stone, until they reached a large round antechamber. Rielle tried to hold her light out enough to light the whole room, and found it was very similar to the chamber in the Temple of Wind.

There was a shallow layer of water that covered the entire floor, and a ring of darker water that ran along the wall, which Rielle assumed meant it was deeper. Vesth looked back and forth warily, motioning for Rielle to wait. He stepped out into the ankle deep water slowly shuffling forward, sweeping his foot with each step to check for hidden obstacles. Finding none, he turned and signaled that it was safe to follow.

Rielle nodded, but then swayed slightly as a hazy vision filled her mind. She gasped and reached out, trying to warn Vesth of danger, but before she said a word Vesth had already seen it. He drew his sword in a blur of motion as a massive shape shot from the water and threw itself at him.

Rielle screamed as an enormous serpent reached out and latched onto Vesth. It's head, nearly as big as a man's torso, bit down into Vesth as he raised his arms to strike and lifted him into the air, trying to wrap itself around him. Vesth quickly reversed his blade and stabbed it deeply into the serpent's neck twisting the blade to cause as much damage as he could.

The serpent let out a gurgling hiss and let Vesth drop to the floor. It retreated slightly, shaking its large head back and forth trying to dislodge the weapon from its jaw. Vesth rolled to his feet and stood still for a few moments before glancing over towards Rielle.

"Run, Rielle." He rasped. "Its not safe." His eyes dimmed and he collapsed to the ground. Rielle covered her mouth with her empty hand, trying not to scream as tears streamed down her face.

She wanted to run to him, to fight, but she could vividly picture the ancient guardian in her mind now. A great two-headed serpent with powerful coils and venomous fangs. She could clearly see yellowish liquid draining from the wounds on Vesth's side. She felt a fire growing in her chest, her tears of fear replaced with ones of anger. She raised her hands above her head and they burst into flames, flickering wildly and lighting every corner of the room.

"Where are you!?" She shouted at the serpent. The wounded head ceased shaking and turned to look directly at her.

It had intelligent, metallic green eyes that mesmerized those who stared too deeply. Rielle, however, was too angry to take notice. She threw one of her fireballs directly into the serpent's face, and watched in surprise as it slid harmlessly over it's smooth scales.

"*You have not the strength of fire to harm these creatures. Not within the walls of the Temple of Water.*" A deep, powerful voice resonated in Rielle's mind. She took a deep, shuddering breath, finally seeing two metallic eyes opposite the first head, peaking from the dark water at the edge of the room.

"Are you the Patriarch?" Rielle asked, not caring if she spoke aloud.

"*Indeed. This is not a battle you can win with the limited magic you have studied thus far.*" Rielle nodded, doing her best to swallow the anger in her throat and listen.

"Then what can I do? I will not leave without him." She looked at Vesth, fighting back more tears. "I refuse to leave without him at my side." A grumble sounded in her mind.

"*You have a duty to perform, and purpose to fulfill. You must not jeopardize that for the sake of one man.*"

"I REFUSE!" Rielle screamed, her voice tearing in her throat. She felt a silent conversation going on in the back of her mind as she wiped tears away from her eyes and continued to stare down the serpent in the chamber, considering throwing another fireball at it. Several tense moments passed.

"*If you will not see reason, then there is only one path left to you.*" The patriarch spoke again. Rielle nodded carefully.

"Whatever it takes, I will do it." Rielle's heart dropped as the Patriarch spoke.

"*Then you must draw me from my scabbard and, with the power of Soaring Zephyr Sidhe, strike down the Guardian.*" Rielle nodded and placed a shaking hand on the hilt of the Patriarch.

"*Do not be afraid.*" Tiasia finally spoke again. "*I will protect you from the worst of the whispers. You will be alright this time. Please be strong, Mister Vesth needs you now.*" Rielle gritted her teeth and nodded. She doused her fire and created another ball of golden light which she sent to hover above the entryway. With another deep breath she pulled the Patriarch from his scabbard and held it before her in both hands.

Whispers immediately filled her mind with chaos. She shook her head, trying to clear it, and felt the whispers lessen.

"*All is well, focus is your strength. The chaos cannot defeat physical form if you do not let it.*" Rielle nodded and tightened her grip on the sword in her hands and looked more closely at the blade to regain her focus.

It was a long, curved blade much like the one master Solidus carried. But the blade itself was more like a steel mosaic stained with blue, red, and copper hues and veined with brilliant silver that ran down the blade like like a bolt of lightning. Rielle felt her mind clear further and turned her attention back to the serpent.

She began to sway back and forth, concentrating her power in her chest as white mist began to gather around her. Time seemed to slow around her and she made a slight twist before planting her foot and racing towards the injured serpent head. Strength filled her limbs as she raised the Patriarch above her head and cut cleanly into the serpent, removing its head.

The serpent's head seemed to slowly drift down through the air, and the water on the floor rose slowly into walls of droplets. But even at this pace, Rielle had only a moment to react as the second serpent head sprang from the water, jaws open wide, fangs extending forward. She quickly stepped forward, kicking off the other head's body to propel her forward.

With a side step and a leap, she pushed herself through the air, spinning several times for momentum before extending her sword and splitting the second head down the middle. She landed and slid to a precarious stop at the edge of the floor and heard the serpent's two heads hitting the floor as the world returned to normal.

Rielle flicked the blood from the blade and, with an unconscious flourish, returned the Patriarch to his scabbard. The remaining whispers faded away and Rielle felt a shiver run down her spine as her power slowed. She rushed, stumbling a little, to Vesth's side and placed one hand against his cheek. He was cold, and pale, the wounds on his side not even bleeding. Rielle faltered and tears returned to her eyes.

For several minutes she knelt beside his body, crying, trying not to lose herself. Then, an idea came to her. She quickly looked around and saw an opening opposite of where they had entered the room. She made a motion, and her light came to rest above her head. She did her best to position herself under Vesth's uninjured side and lifted him, half dragging him towards the opening.

As she had suspected, once they passed through the opening,

she found herself at the edge of a great seal, at the center of which stood a glowing blue altar. Rielle dragged Vesth to the altar and laid him down carefully. Then she knelt beside the Altar, clasped her hands together, and rested her arms on its surface.

She reached out with her mind, looking for a presence, asking for an audience. After what seemed like hours to Rielle, the glow of the altar grew brighter and suddenly the air around her felt thick and heavy.

"Who Enters My Temple?" A loud voice thundered around the room, shaking everything.

"Great Titan Perion. I am Rielle Toriel Lyvinius. I am a student of Silver Mage Pravin Solidus, here to ask for your aid."

"So You Are The One Then. The One Of Which The Balance Mage Spoke." Rielle nodded her head.

"Yes. I came here to ask for your blessing, so that I might continue my battle with the chaos knowing I stand under the protection of the Great Titan." There were several more moments of silence and then the Diety of Water spoke again.

"You Ask For My Blessing, You Say To Battle The Chaos. But I Sense A Distraction, A Wavering Of Your Faith In Me." Rielle hurriedly shook her head.

"No, of course not. I have utmost Faith in you, Great Titan Perion. It's just.." Rielle faultered.

"Yes?" The rumble was not quite as loud as it had been before.

"It's just that My friend, My protector, has fallen injured. He is on the verge of death, and I have not the skill to heal him myself." Rielle fought back tears as she spoke, not wanting to lose control at such an important moment.

"I see." The voice was still powerful, but it no longer rumbled or shook the floor. "You had hoped that, along with my blessing, you would ask that he be saved." Rielle nodded.

"You are indeed wise and all seeing Great Perion. He has been with me since I began this journey. I draw strength from him, and I fear that I would not be able to fulfill my duty without him." A few more moments of silence.

"I will not heal him." Rielle's breath caught in her throat, but she bowed her head more deeply behind the altar to hide it.

"But I will Grant you my Cloak, with which you may heal him yourself." Rielle's head shot up, a few tears escaping her eyes.

"Thank you." She nearly sobbed. "You are truly most benevolent and kind. A being worthy of the highest respect and praise." The air grew heavier and the Temple shook.

"Then Accept My Cloak Mortal, And Carry Forth The Will Of Perion Into This World Once More." Rielle nearly fell back from the altar as she was hit with a blast of power that felt like a wave crashing over her. She squeezed her eyes shut and did her best to stay upright. Shortly after, she felt the weight lift from her and her eyes blinked open.

The altar was now dark, the glowing having transferred itself to surround her body. She lifted her hands and saw they were covered in a thin layer of water. The aches of previous days, and the tiredness of using the Cloak of Sidhe, faded away beneath the cool water.

Rielle stood and carefully made her way to Vesth's side and knelt again. She placed her hands against the two open wounds and watched in wonder as the water on her hands flowed into the wound and carried out the toxic venom.

Broken ribs and flesh repaired themselves and the skin closed over the holes still left behind. Vesth gasped in air, and released a ragged breath, his face returning to normal color. The glow around Rielle faded, and the water fell from her hands. She reached out and placed a hand on Vesth's face and a relieved smile touched her lips.

She lifted him and half carried, half dragged him to the bottom of the stone stairs. After a few moments of thought, she carefully leaned him against the wall and raced up the stairs, catching herself a few times to keep from slipping back down. She exited the Temple and raced to the shore where she jumped and waved until she got Keliter's attention.

He leaped onto his horse and rushed down to meet her. Once she had explained what happened, and assured him that The Deity of Water was gone, he followed her into the Temple and helped her carry Vesth back up to the horses. They returned to their small camp and laid Vesth down to rest on his bed roll.

Rielle fell back onto her own bed shuddering from the stress of everything that had just happened. She laid there, quietly contemplating, only speaking just as the sun was setting.

"I am sorry Keliter." The Telatian shifted from his place by the fire.

"Oh? Do you have anything to be sorry for?" Rielle nodded, staring into the blue and orange sky.

"I... Treated you poorly, even though I had no logical reason to do so." Keliter chuckled.

"I was once the personal servant of your sworn enemy. You have every right to be suspicious of my intent." Rielle sighed.

"I still should have been more temperate in my response. I

sense in you no ill will towards anyone, and yet I still treated you like a potential enemy. For that I apologize. I am glad you came with us." She felt his gaze turn to her and waited for a few moments to hear his response.

"Thank you. I am honored that you have allowed me to stay with you on this journey." Rielle smiled.

"We will rest here until Vesth wakes again. Then we leave for Tiamat's Cave."

7

Chapter Seven

Rielle sat quietly in her saddle as the Serpent's Tongue steadily passed them by. She played the scenes of her journey over and over through her mind, hoping to see all the mistakes she had made, hoping to learn from them.

Her eyes kept drifting towards Vesth, riding a few paces ahead of her. He had insisted he was fine to ride, though he was still stiff from the day before. His posture told her he was still riding steady, and she tried to focus her attention elsewhere and stop worrying. She continued to sort through her thoughts, pushing back to earlier and earlier memories, filing everything away in her mind to be recalled later if necessary.

She was so engaged in this task that her breath caught in surprise when she found herself remembering her mother's face. She noticed Vesth glance at her over his shoulder, and she smiled to let him know that everything was fine.

"Does it still hurt to remember?" Tiasia asked quietly. Rielle sat silently for several moments before answering.

"I am not sure that hurt is the right word. I mean, I used to think that is what I was feeling. But thinking over it now, I am not sure it actually was. Maybe I felt betrayed or exposed or... or..."

"Guilty?" Rielle felt a lump in her throat and tried to swallow it.

"Why was I put in such a position? What was I meant to do?" Rielle could almost feel Tiasia put her small arms around her comfortingly.

"You shouldn't feel guilty about what happened. You were so young then, nobody could have expected anything from you." Rielle shook her head.

"Then why? Why would they do such a thing to their daughter?" There was a moment of internal silence before she got an answer.

"There is someone here you could ask." Without even having to ask, Rielle's eyes drifted to Keliter's back. Then her eyes turned to Vesth.

"Do you not trust mister Vesth?" Rielle frowned.

"It's not that, I just..." She could feel Tiasia nodding.

"You can't hold everything in forever. The questions you have will only wear at you until you can think of nothing else. Would it not be better to tell him, and maybe get some closure?" Rielle felt her lip tremble slightly.

"But what if I really was some sort of..."

"You won't ever know unless you ask. And even if it were true, Mister Vesth won't think any differently of you." Rielle shook

herself trying to keep her thoughts clear. She looked at Vesth, then to Keliter and back to Vesth again. Finally she sighed.

"Keliter, might I pose a question?" Keliter glanced over his shoulder and slowed his horse a bit.

"If you wish." He replied simply. Vesth also looked back at her with a questioning look. Rielle took a deep breath to calm her nerves.

"May I ask how you know of my past?" Keliter smiled knowingly.

"I see. The answer is that I was in Terramine during the events." Rielle's eyes widened and Keliter nodded. "I was not very old, maybe fifteen, but old enough to be allowed into the circle."

"So you were part of the Cult that was trying to assimilate into the city?" Keliter nodded again.

"I was, though I did leave their ranks shortly after turning eighteen. So I was never fully integrated into the social structure." Rielle nodded.

"I understand. Then would you know..." Keliter raised one eyebrow as Rielle looked uncomfortably at Vesth. Vesth noticed immediately.

"I can ride ahead if you wish." He said, lifting his reigns. Rielle quickly shook her head.

"No, its ok Vesth... I... I just haven't spoken about it out loud before. It's against Hortaal Law to speak of what happened. As it pertained to the royal family, but... I want to know why it happened."

"Aaah." Keliter said, understanding dawning on him. "I see. You were very young and likely were never told the entire story." Rielle nodded.

"I know most of what happened, the basics anyway. I just never knew why they did what they did to me." Vesth slowed his horse until he was riding even with Rielle.

"Are you sure it is alright for me to hear?" Rielle nodded.

"My cousin, the High King, won't mind if I am discreet and you don't speak of it to anyone else." Vesth watched her for a few moments and then nodded.

"You had a question, but if Vesth is to hear it, perhaps it would be wise to tell the whole story so he will not misunderstand." Keliter spoke quietly. Rielle nodded.

"That may be for the best." Keliter nodded.

"Then perhaps you should begin. Tell us what you know and remember, and I will do my best to fill in the gaps." Rielle nodded and took a shaky breath. She felt Tiasia place a small hand on her shoulder and tried to quiet her doubts.

"When I was very young, around three or four, my mother and father came forward and claimed that I was the Reincarnation of some sort of powerful being. Possibly an angel or demon, or even High King Hortaal himself by some accounts. They used this as an excuse to try and remove my Uncle, Maron Ralith Toriel, from the throne of Hortaal and put me in his place.

They tried for weeks to gather support for this motion, But my Uncle was a well loved king and no one wanted to see him removed. So eventually my Father enlisted the aid of a group of people who claimed they could prove to the people that I was truly Hortaal Reborn. They said that, once it was proven, the High King himself would even step down to make way for me. In return they wanted to be allowed to live in the city and some of them were to be given positions of power in my court.

They gathered in the center of town and attracted a huge crowd. But the 'proof' the group had promised turned out to be magic. They intended to cast a spell of some sort to show I was a powerful being. But It backfired. Hatred of magic is so ingrained in Hortaal that the moment this group of people attempted to use their power, the crowd turned on them in an instant. Most of them were taken, or stoned, on the spot.

They captured my father, but my mother managed to take me and carry me back to the palace where she hid me away in our room. But a mob had formed and they came to the palace demanding that Me and my mother be turned over. My Uncle took custody of my father and locked him away in the dungeon along with my mother. My Uncle's court wished to have me imprisoned as well, but my Cousin Morien stayed at my side the entire night and would not let them take me.

Eventually the court ruled that I was too young to hold any responsibility for what had happened, And I was spared when my mother and father were sentenced to death." Vesth's eyes widened at this. Rielle nodded.

"I was only recently informed that Master Solidus even came down from the Mercury Mountains to see events unfold and that My cousin was the one who made the proclamation as High Prince that I was innocent." Vesth nodded, clearly thinking carefully over everything he had heard.

"That is what I know of what happened. Is there anything else you can add Keliter?" Keliter nodded.

"There is, but I would like to hear your original question first." Rielle resisted the urge to bite her lip.

"Why did they choose me? What made them think I was

something besides human?" Keliter nodded quietly for a few moments before answering.

"Greed." Rielle blink in surprise at this answer.

"Greed?" Keliter nodded again.

"Yes. Your story was a good summary, but it is not quite correct. Your Father did not meet our cult after the fact. He had been involved with them for months before even coming up with the plan. He wanted into the cult, so that he could gain the power that our priests claimed to have. But they wanted something in return. They wanted power within the city, so that they could eventually take over.

He came up with the idea of putting you on the throne, and then ruling as your steward until you came of age. That way he could appoint them to the court and give them other governing positions throughout the kingdom.

He knew all along that they were magic users, but when he failed to convince the people of the kingdom that you should be placed on the throne, he turned to them once again, promising anything they wanted in return for their help.

They planned on making it seem as if the ghost of High King Hortaal was rising from your body and inspire people to believe it was true. But they underestimated the response to magic that the people of Terramine would have, and many of them died before being able to escape the city. It took a great deal of convincing for that mob to believe the High King when he told them that you had not been tainted by the magic." Rielle nodded, not sure if she was relieved or not hearing Keliter's answer to her question.

She didn't have much time to think it over though, because something on the horizon caught her attention and a broad smile covered her face at the same time a tear rolled down her cheek. Vesth gave her a strange look then followed her gaze, a smile touching one corner of his mouth when he saw what she was looking at.

* * *

Segine waved excitedly as the three people on horseback drew closer. Nysisset stood beside him, doing her best to look indifferent, though she still smiled.

Rielle rushed forward, almost at a gallop, and stopped next to them, leaping from her horse and throwing her arms around Nysisset.

"I am so happy to see you two alive!" She cried, tears of joy in her eyes. Vesth rode up, followed by a man in sand colored clothing, and climbed down from his horse as well. He and Segine clasped arms, the knight grinning broadly.

"You are a sight for sore eyes." Segine said, a little over loud. "We had heard from Master Delgorin that all was going well with you, but it is still good to see you in one piece all the same." Vesth nodded, finally smiling fully.

"And seeing that you survived that foolish leap off the ship is most reassuring." Segine chuckled a little awkwardly, scratching the back of his head.

"I may have made a rash decision."

"When do you not?" Nysisset asked pointedly, finally getting out of Rielle's hug. Vesth glanced at her, but she didn't actually seem as angry as she was trying to sound. Rielle turned her head to one side and looked at Segine's left arm.

"What happened to your arm Segine?" Segine glanced at what looked like a burn on his forearm.

"I... uh..." Nysisset let out an aggravated sigh.

"We met a Demon host three nights ago. Segine borrowed my power to fight the creature and when the night was over it left its mark on him." Segine nodded, a bit dejected.

"Three nights ago? Was that not also when we met with the Basilisk?" The man in the Sand colored clothes spoke. Vesth nodded.

"I believe so." Nysisset scowled.

"It seems our enemy grows wary of us. Perhaps he realizes we may yet beat him."

"Borsa has known the threat you pose to him since the beginning." They all turned, the men with their hands on their swords, to find Delgorin sitting high up on a rock ledge, eating a small red fruit.

"I see that you still like to sneak up on people old man." Nysisset grumbled. The old man grinned and disappeared, reappearing next to them.

"I only go where I am told." He said mischievously.

"That doesn't seem likely." Nysisset responded with a frown.

"Master Delgorin." Rielle said with a slight bow. "I assume that when Master Solidus said things would be explained to us here, he meant he would send you to tell us what we need to do next." Delgorin nodded, a little more mellow now.

"Indeed he did miss." Rielle frowned slightly.

"You are going to ask us to split up again, aren't you?" Delgorin nodded again.

"You are correct, miss Rielle. Though you should not worry, as you will be separated only a short time. The end of our conflict draws very near." Segine puffed out his chest.

"Then let us be done with this quest. What news bring you from Master Solidus?" Delgorin grinned.

"You, my good knight, will be going with young Nysisset to speak with Necrotic Dracolich Khornal." Segine seemed to deflate, sputtering slightly. Nysisset shot him a poisonous glance and he silenced himself.

"You will go along with Rielle to speak with Lord Tiamat, who will send you on your way." Delgorin said, motioning with his half eaten fruit towards the cave entrance.

"I need to speak with Lord Tiamat then?" Rielle said, looking a bit uncomfortable. Delgorin nodded with a knowing smile.

"Indeed. The pilgrims path is a long journey, but we are short on time now. You have the Cloak of Sidhe and the Cloak of Perion. If you are to be at your strongest when you face the final conflict, you must balance yourself and Gain the Cloak of Pariah and the Cloak of Railast. The fastest way to complete that task is to ask Tiamat to show you the way to the Temple of Fire.

From there, after speaking with Blazing Pheonix Pariah, you will be shown the way to the Temple of Earth." Rielle nodded.

"I understand." Delgorin's smile faded.

"However, I must warn you, You will be making this last part of your journey alone." Rielle felt her breath catch in her throat. Delgorin turned to Vesth.

"Solidus asked that you remain here with me until the others have gone. Then I am to give you instructions for what you are to do. After that task, you are to meet the Combined armies of the Three Kingdoms and help lead them to the place Solidus will reveal to you. The Knight and Miss Nysisset will meet you there as well." Delgorin then turned to Keliter.

"And don't think you will be left out either. I am to inform you that you will be heading to the Great Southwestern Gate. You will be under the direct command of High King Morien." Keliter nodded, accepting his assignment.

"And there is no other way?" Rielle asked. Delgorin turned to face her, sparing a moment to search her expression.

"I'm afraid not. But as I said, you will not be separated for long. In fact, if all goes well, it may be only a matter of a few days before you are all reunited." Rielle nodded slowly, her eyes glazing slightly. Vesth hesitated for a few moments, then placed a hand on her shoulder.

"You are strong enough." She looked up into his eyes and he met her gaze.

"You are the only one who can convince the remaining of The Six to aid us. From all I have seen and heard of you on our travels, I know you will be alright. And we all support you, even when we are parted." Rielle felt another hand on her shoulder and turned to see Nysisset, her expression oddly gentle.

"I agree with Vesth. You are that which binds us all together, and we are with you one hundred percent. If you need us we will come running to help you. No matter what the stuffy old man tells us." She shot a glance over her shoulder at Delgorin who simply stood by with a large grin on his face. Rielle smiled

"Thank you, All of you." Vesth nodded, and Nysisset did the same before turning back to Delgorin.

"Is that all you are meant to tell us Old Man?" Delgorin's grin widened.

"I think we've covered everything."

"Good." Nysisset stated shortly. She grabbed her pack from her saddle and, taking hold of Rielle's hand, lead her towards the cave opening.

"I will enjoy having someone to speak with other than the hardheaded knight for a change." Rielle followed along with a quick glance back at Vesth. Vesth chuckled quietly.

"You seem to have had quite the journey." He said, looking at the knight. Segine frowned and shook his head.

"I would not know where to begin." Vesth pulled Rielle's pack from her horse and held it out to Segine.

"We can tell our tales once we are done with our duties." Segine took Rielle's pack with a nod, and shouldered his own.

"Indeed, I will throw a banquet at my home where we may speak long and freely and forget about our hardships." Vesth smiled and clasped hands again with the knight.

"I would be honored to accept the invitation." Segine grinned broadly and then turned to follow Nysisset and Rielle.

"Then we will make it a feast to make all in the Three King-doms envious." Vesth nodded and watched him go.

"I too will take my leave then." Vesth heard Keliter say from behind him. He turned and saw the Telatian mounting his horse again.

"Then I will see you when I meet with the armies." Keliter nodded and sat silently. Vesth watched the man for a few moments before reaching out his hand. Keliter seemed mildly surprised for a moment then accepted his handshake.

"Until we meet once more." He said, looking down from his horse, a smile touching his lips.

"Until we meet once more." Vesth responded before taking a step back and watching Keliter start on the path down the mountain. He watched for a moment then spoke.

"I suppose you were meant to tell me my task only after everyone else had left because it will be dangerous and Master

Solidus did not wish Rielle to worry." He turned to face Delgorin, who nodded with a somber look on his face.

"You are sharp as ever young one." Delgorin stepped forward and held out a small envelope. Vesth took it and inspected it.

"I do not recognize this seal." He said motioning to the blob of wax that sealed the envelope closed. Delgorin nodded slowly.

"It is the Seal of Alenon. A letter from High Priest Agamemnon. You are meant to deliver it for him." Vesth looked up at the old man, waiting for the part he knew he wouldn't like. Delgorin turned away and stared, as if through the mountain itself.

"It is a plea for safety. It is to be delivered to the Queen of Fairies within Telatia." Vesth felt his stomach turn over.

"Master Solidus said that the Fairies were driven mad. That any who encountered them in the desert would also be driven mad." Delgorin nodded.

"Or killed, most likely." Vesth took a slow breath to keep himself calm.

"Then how am I to deliver this letter?" Delgorin was silent for a few moments.

"Make no mistake, this will likely be the most danger you have ever found yourself in. But without the amnesty of the fairies, all of the army that marches into Telatia will never march back out again. Bare that in mind, keep your focus, and use your key." Vesth unconsciously reached down and felt a small object in a pouch at his side.

"I have never used it for an extended period of time before." Delgorin turned to face him again.

"You must maintain a constant output of energy, and keep

your mind as empty as possible. Focus on ensuring your power flows through you in a loop, always returning to it's source. If you feel your control waning, and the voices press against your mind, open another gate. If all else fails, focus on your desire to protect Rielle, and remember that you must survive this to be able to help her." Vesth Jaw tightened.

"Then where must I go?" Delgorin placed a hand on Vesth's shoulder.

"I will show you." The air shimmered around them, and then they were gone, leaving only four horses grazing quietly on the mountainside.

* * *

Segine hesitated for a moment inside the narrow passageway that opened into the large chamber before him. He could see Nysisset and Rielle talking quietly in the center of the chamber, Rielle occasionally laughing at whatever story Nysisset was telling her.

"There is no sense hiding in the dark little one." Segine stiffened as he heard the deep grumbling voice. "I was already awakened by Master Solidus." Segine slowly stepped inside the chamber, scanning around to find a tall, slim man with long red hair leaning against the wall.

"The young ones there seem to be well at ease, yet your mind strays to times past." Segine half bowed.

"I find it difficult not to think of my previous experience here." The red haired man nodded slowly, as if groggy or tired.

"I will admit I was a bit ill tempered when Master Solidus brought you through my domain. He had broken a serious magical law, and woke me from my rest." The man paused a moment to yawn.

"I apologize for disturbing you further." Segine apologized. The man waved his hand.

"It is of little concern. Borsa's actions are stirring up the spirits in the sands beyond the mountains, and their howling makes any sleep difficult." The man yawned again and pushed himself away from the wall.

"So if you could all deal with him in a timely manner so that I may return to my rest, I would be grateful." Segine nodded.

"I believe that is the plan." The man nodded and started off towards the two women and Segine followed. As he approached them, Rielle and Nysisset turned and bowed. Nysisset more stiffly than Rielle.

"We were to ask for your aid, Great Tiamat." Rielle said as she straightned. The red haired man nodded.

"Yes, I am aware. Master Solidus filled me in, in great detail." Rielle nodded in return, a slight smile touching her lips.

"Then what do you wish us to do? Hopefully we may not inconvenience you overmuch, and allow you to return to your slumber." Tiamat nodded tiredly.

"Indeed. Normally I would test you extensively, Miss Rielle, to see if you are worthy of entering Lady Pariah's Temple." Rielle waited apprehensively as Tiamat scratched his head in thought. She was surprised to see a smile tug at one corner of his mouth.

"Though I did enjoy hearing of you putting that self righteous Queztacoatl in her place." The dragon in human form chuckled with a deep rumble in his chest.

"So perhaps I can make an exception. I was also instructed to send the Knight and the Changeling to meet with Lord

Khornal. To do so I would be sending them through a ring portal. I hear you are familiar with them." Rielle nodded slowly.

"I believe so. Is it like the one on the highest peak of the Mercury Mountains? The one that leads to the High Temple of Alenon?" Tiamat nodded.

"Indeed, though the portals of Alenon are activated through light. This one is activated through the use of fire."

"I see. Then yes, I am familiar with them." Tiamat grinned.

"Then open it for me, and I will consider allowing you to enter the Temple of Fire." He raised his hand and snapped his fingers. A rumbling, grinding sound echoed throughout the cavern and a set of rings covered in fiery red gems rose from one of the glowing pits. Heat flowed from the steps around the rings in waves that made the area around them seem to warp and twist. Tiamat motioned towards the rings.

"At your leisure, little one." Rielle nodded and turned to Nysisset and Segine.

"Are you ready to go?" Both nodded.

"Yes, it will be good to breathe the air of the mountains again." Nysisset said, a bit wistfully. Segine held out Rielle's pack, and she took it.

"When we are done in the mountains, we will be making our way back to meet with the army. We will be waiting for you there." Rielle nodded, a lump in her throat preventing her from speaking. Nysisset reached out and squeezed her hand.

"Hurry and return to us. Vesth will be with us too, and then we will finish what we started." Rielle smiled with a sniffle, and wiped a tear from her eye.

"Of course, be well until then." Nysisset smiled.

"I will be well enough if the knight can keep his mouth

shut." Rielle laughed as Segine grumbled and frowned. Rielle placed her pack on the ground and walked across the cavern until she came to the set of rings. She closed her eyes breathing in slow, measured breaths, before half turning and raising her hands in the air.

The ground began to shake, small rocks on the floor of the cavern skittering along the uneven stone. The air around Rielle began to ripple and warp, rising in a plume towards the ceiling. Then fire began to rise from the numerous glowing holes in the floor, flowing like rivers of liquid heat that encircled her.

Rielle's body began to glow with a faint purple aura as she gathered the fire around her until she was surrounded with a swirling pillar of flame. Several moments went by, then she shifted her feet and twisted her arms around her, the fire reacting to her as if it were tied to her limbs. With a lifting and pushing motion, she forced the fire to draw down around her and flow up her arms and shoot into the gems in the rings before her.

With a groan of protest the rings loosened and began to move, spinning faster and faster as the flames fed into them. Eventually the rings were humming smoothly and seemed to be a single, molten red disk. Rielle slid her feet together and straightened her back, raising her hands above her head.

"The portal is open." She called over the loud hum. Segine found he had been staring in amazement and shook himself, Nysisset glaring at him impatiently.

Segine quickly walked forward, Nysisset close behind, and rushed towards the disk. He faltered slightly as he approached, but Nysisset pushed up behind him, propelling him through the portal and out of sight.

Rielle slowly moved her hands together above her head, then slid one foot behind her and swept her hands down and back, as if bowing. The power rushed from the portal and flowed back down into the holes in the floor.

The humming slowly died down and the rings ground to a halt. Rielle stood, sweeping her hands before her as she calmed her inner power. She swayed a little and shuddered. Slow clapping echoed around the now quiet cavern.

"Consider me impressed." Tiamat said, applauding for a moment before his hands returned to his sides. "For one so young, you have grown remarkably." Rielle tiredly bowed.

"Thank you, you honor me with your words. I do not feel I deserve such praise." Tiamat lifted Rielle's pack and walked to her side, holding it out to her.

"There are few I have seen who command fire with the dedication and grace you have just shown. You take to the magic as one who was born in the flames." Rielle gratefully accepted her pack, and placed it over her shoulders.

"Master Solidus once told me something like that. That I was first taught in the Heaven Realm to use my power before being born into the world." Tiamat tipped his head to one side to inspect her.

"Antiquorum Anima Mea... Then perhaps Born of Flame is not far off." He mumbled.

"Antiqu..." Rielle started to speak, but Tiamat cut her off with a wave.

"It is nothing. But it is clear that the young Master Solidus is uniquely aware of details that elude the rest of us." Rielle could see fire dancing in the dragon's eyes.

"Perhaps it is time I left my cave to speak at length with the

Silver Mage." Rielle shifted a little uncomfortably, not wanting to interrupt the dragon's line of thought again. Tiamat stood quietly for a few more moments before seemingly remembering Rielle was there.

"Perhaps you are worthy to enter the Temple of Fire." He said quietly, all the tiredness he had shown before, seemed to have disappeared.

"I will show you the way, I leave the final decision to Blazing Pheonix Pariah." Rielle bowed wordlessly. The dragon nodded to her and then turned, walking towards the far wall.

As he walked he raised his arms and weaved an intricate pattern in the air, light trailing from his fingertips. The wall began to shimmer and dissolve leading out onto a lush prairie. Rielle followed in wonder, steep mountain cliffs raising on either side of her, cool air rushing past her. The afternoon sun shone down on the green grass, and reflecting off scattered pools of water.

"Where are we?" Rielle asked, marveling at her surroundings.

"We are in the far northeastern end of Telatia." Tiamat stated, waving his arms again to close the portal behind them. Rielle blinked in surprise.

"What you see before you is what all of Telatia once was. A paradise of lush plants that teem with life." Rielle stared blankly around her.

"This was Telatia?" Tiamat nodded.

"Before the demons got their claws into it, and Master Solidus had to remove them by force." Rielle felt her heart aching.

"It used to be so beautiful, the fairies dancing among the

trees and ponds were the most beautiful creatures on the face of Galbrea." Rielle could feel Tiasia sigh sadly.

"How did this place escape distruction?" Rielle asked. Tiamat glanced over his shoulder at her.

"It didn't." Rielle stared blankly, not comprehending. Tiamat grumbled.

"How does Master Solidus deal with such constant questioning?" Rielle averted her gaze.

"I'm sorry." The dragon sighed.

"Don't be, you are young, and would not understand such things. This place became corrupted the same as the rest of Telatia, and as such was torn apart and banished into the void. But this valley houses the Temple of Fire. Fire fuels all life in this world." Rielle nodded.

"I remember Master Solidus teaching me that. We are made of earth, willed to life by fire, and sustained by water and air." Rielle watched Tiamat's red hair seem to light ablaze as it waved in the sunlight as he nodded.

"Indeed, and this valley is in the mountains very close to the sea. The winds from the plains draw moisture and seedlings over the mountains and it settles here. The power of the Temple of Fire radiates across the valley and gives strength to those small bits of life that began to grow. Now it has become very close to what it used to be, though the Fairies have yet to return. Their grief over their lost home is too long lived, and it twists their hearts." Rielle stared sadly at the grass beneath her feet.

"And there is nothing that can be done for them?" Tiamat paused, slowing his stride until he came to a stop.

"Not in hundreds of years have I heard another who voiced

such empathy for them. Not since Siguard Agamemnon has any hoped to help them." Rielle looked up in surprise.

"Agamemnon sought to help the fairies?" Tiamat nodded.

"He was here when Solidus destroyed Telatia, Shielding the Temple of Fire to ensure no damage was done where it would do more harm. Many fairies were corrupted and had to be destroyed, but the Queen and those in her grotto were protected from the destruction, as her power was pure enough to protect them. But their homeland, once called Teine Fearann, was destroyed beyond recognition.

The Queen knew what would have happened if the corruption had been allowed to fester, but even so, her grief and that of her people was so great that they were blinded to all reason. Many of those who died refused to pass on, and their spirits roam, hoping to make all others they find suffer the same grief that they do." Rielle felt a lump forming in her throat and she squeezed her hands into tight fists.

"If we are able to destroy Borsa and the demons he has called to this world, will we be able to save those fairies who remain? Will we be able to begin the process of healing their grief?" Tiamat looked her up and down, inspecting her features before turning and walking towards the other end of the valley again.

"If you succeed, then perhaps there is hope for them." Rielle stared at her balled up fists, breathing deeply.

"I will not fail. For all those who have been hurt by Borsa and all his kind I will fight to bring them closure and justice." She released her fists and followed after Tiamat once more.

"I will not fail."

8

Chapter Eight

Segine felt as if the Deity of Evil was staring straight through him as he casually sipped at his wine glass.

"You seem to be no worse for wear." The Deity said with a grin. "I assume you had no adverse reactions to my power?" Segine grumbled unhappily.

"Not as much as I had expected." He replied, averting his eyes from Nysisset's glare. Khornal chuckled before sitting forward in his throne.

"There is something I would ask you before we discuss your arrangement." Segine nodded.

"I will do my best to answer." Khornal nodded in return.

"Good. Then I wish to know how your Grandfather is doing." Segine blinked in surprise.

"My... Grandfather?" Khornal nodded again.

"Yes. Marion Carsolia Memoria." Segine glanced at Nysisset

who continued to glare and motion for him to answer. Segine cleared his throat before speaking.

"My Grandfather was killed in an 'accident' during a tournament several years ago." Khornal's dark eyes searched Segine's face.

"Killed? But you don't believe for a moment it was an accident, do you?" Segine scowled.

"Not a knight in the realm thought it was an accident, not for a moment. But the investigation after found no evidence pointing to deliberate murder. The Knight King ruled it as an accident." Khornal slowly sat back in his throne, his wine glass vanishing into the dark shadows around him.

"What happened?" Segine glanced back at Nysisset. Her glare was gone, replaced with confusion and curiosity.

"He was in a jousting match with another knight. He unseated his opponent, but when his charger came to a stop he toppled from his saddle. His armor was cracked open as if brittle, and the broken lance of his opponent had found its way inside." Khornal stared intently as Segine spoke.

"And none had tampered with his armor?" Segine shook his head.

"In tournaments the Knight King provides all weapons and armor to the knights so that none may tamper with the items, or bring weapons that give an unfair advantage. The armor and weapons were checked thoroughly and the rest of my Grand-fathers armor was properly tempered, and did not break when struck." Khornal nodded again, still staring intently.

"And how was he buried?" Segine turned his head to one side in confusion.

"He was interred in our family tomb at my estate by my

Father. Why?" Khornal sat quietly for several long moments, his eyes staring through Segine into some distant place.

"His soul has not returned to me." Segine blinked in surprise before remembering what the Deity had told him in the plains.

"Should he have immediately returned once he died?" Khornal nodded slowly.

"Provided his body had not been ill treated after death, which you tell me it has not. It is suspicious that he has not returned per our contract." Segine stood silently for several seconds before what was said sank in.

"Contract?" Khornal turned his gaze back to Segine.

"Indeed. Almost every Generation of the Memoria bloodline has made a contract with me. Your Grandfather included." Segine stood stunned, staring blankly at the Deity on his throne. Khornal leaned forward in his throne again.

"I have always had need of Black Knights, sworn to my service, who act as my hunters when evil begins to sprout outside the confines of the Mercury Mountains. In return for my power, they await until I send them forth to return what belongs to me. Or to hunt down souls who seek to avoid my gaze after death." Segine slowly tried to think over this information.

"What of my Father?" Khornal shook his head.

"I pass my power to only one knight at any time. When the soul of my Black Knight passes, I make contact with his descendant to make a new contract. As your Grandfather's soul never passed, I never made a contract with your father. But that matters little now. Who opposed your grandfather in the Tournament?" Segine shook himself to clear his head and then shrugged.

"I do not know. I was still training at my Father's estate at the time. I was only given the news when I was told to make ready for his funeral." Khornal rested his elbows on his knees and laced his fingers together in thought. Segine stood uncomfortably, waiting for the Deity to speak again.

"Nysisset." Khornal said, and Nysisset bowed. "Go to the spring and bring me a drop of mercury." Nysisset bowed more deeply and then turned, disappearing into the caves behind them. Once she was gone, Khornal stood and stepped down from his throne to stand eye to eye with Segine.

"Will you carry on your bloodline's legacy? Will you forge a contract with me?" Segine set his jaw and squared his shoulders.

"What are the terms?" Khornal locked eyes with the knight, not allowing him to look away.

"You will be at my beck and call. You will hunt the souls of the dead who will not pass. You will seek out Evil wherever it may be found and return it to me. You will protect my servant Nysisset until the end of your days, whether she wants you to or not. And lastly..." Khornal paused and leaned in close to the knight, finishing with a spiteful whisper.

"You will find the one who slayed my knight, and you will end him." Segine shuddered as he felt the Deity's Malice creep down his spine.

"And in return you will give me the power I need?" Khornal took a step back.

"And more, Knight. Much, much more." Segine took a deep breath, carefully quelling the doubts rising within him.

"I find these terms acceptable, so long as I am permitted to act as I see fit." Khornal deliberately eyed the knight up and down before holding out his hand.

"Then we have a deal?" Segine looked down at the deity's hand before reaching out and firmly grasping it with his own.

"I swear by blood and by name that I, Segine Memoria, will fulfill my duties as agreed." A grin slowly crept onto Khornal's face as he shook Segine's hand. Segine heard a scuff on the cave floor behind him and Khornal held out his empty hand, still tightly gripping Segine's with his other.

Nysisset carefully stepped up beside them and held out her two cupped hands. Sitting in them was a large drop of liquid silver metal, shimmering in the dim light provided by the fires around them. Khornal reached out his hand and the drop rose into the air.

"Then I, Khornal, Deity of Darkness, agree to our terms. I welcome you into my fold, and Brand you as my own." With a sudden twist, Khornal grasped the floating silver drop and smashed it. Dark shadows poured from his hand as the silver oozed from between his fingers.

Then, with agonizing purpose, he reached out and clasped his hand onto Segine's shoulder. Pain like nothing Segine had ever felt before blinded him and he felt his knees hit the floor. The pain spread from his shoulder, down his arm, and almost down to his wrist before it finally stopped. Segine sat on the floor for several minutes, gasping for air.

When he was finally able to breath freely he raised his head and looked around. The cave no longer seemed as dark as it had been, the fires burned brightly, lighting the room and everything in it save for a dense darkness behind Khornal himself.

Nysisset knelt beside him, with one hand on his shoulder to support him. He looked up at her and, for what felt like the first time, noticed how well her violet eyes matched her raven hair. Segine heard an amused chuckle and turned to see Khornal sitting down on his throne before once again conjuring his wine glass.

"Now we shall see how well you perform, my Black Knight." Segine bowed his head then struggled to his feet.

"What would you have me do?" Khornal swirled his glass before taking a sip.

"For now, you should simply return to what you were doing before. Solidus knows what needs to be done, simply follow his instructions as you would my own." Segine bowed alongside Nysisset, though he heard her grumbling. Khornal grinned widely.

"Just remember the conditions of your contract. There will be plenty of opportunities for you to fulfill them where you are going." With this said, the Deity slowly dissolved away into a cloud of black mist that vanished into the darkness.

They stood quietly for several moments before Segine turned to Nysisset. But as he opened his mouth to speak to her, she placed a finger against his lips and shook her head.

"Nothing needs to be said, knight. You have accepted your contract and gained the power we need to fight against the demonic forces of Borsa." She paused for another moment and then smiled at him and let her finger fall back to her side.

"I'm proud of you. For choosing this path, even though you had wished not to." Segine's jaw tightened, but he managed a weak smile and a nod. Nysisset laughed at him.

"Welcome to the fold Segine. Now lets go take Borsa down

a peg." Segine felt his smile grow as she turned away, and he followed close behind.

"At least on that, we can agree."

* * *

Vesth stared emptily at a cave entrance, his mind a blank slate as the power from his first gate pounded in his ears. He could hear voices like small bells singing wordlessly within it's depths, and the sound of running water humming beneath them.

Vesth glanced over his shoulder once more, hoping to see Delgorin waiting for him. But the old man had disappeared shortly after bringing him to this cave in the desert, leaving him to fulfill his task alone.

Vesth shook his head, trying to drive away the unwanted thoughts. He reached into a small pouch at his side and pulled out a smooth, uneven, translucent stone. He raised it to eye level, focusing into its depths, and gradually opened his second gate. The tide of power flowed through him, warming every corner of his being. He placed the stone back in his pouch, and began moving forward into the cave, carefully directing his focus into the even beating of his power.

Light emanated from the cave walls, lighting his way through the jagged black stone. After several minutes of walking he began to see movements. Only out of the corner of his eyes at first, and nothing solid, but slowly the motions began to take form.

Small human-like shapes, as if formed from mist, drifted back and forth through the walls. Whispers, coaxing him to follow them drifted to Vesth's ears, but their faces were split by twisted, spiteful grins. Vesth's jaw tightened and he felt his hand drifting towards the smooth stone at his side.

He resisted the urge to groan as the power from his third gate filled him with an immense pressure. As he struggled to maintain a steady pace, he found himself walking into a large open cavern. In the center of the cavern was a large, clear pool with water dripping down from various cracks in the ceiling above. Within the pool itself was a large crystal formation that glowed with otherworldly light that reached into every corner.

Vesth could feel many eyes watching his approach as he neared the pool. Not knowing what else to do, he simply stood beside the pool and watched the ripples in the water, waiting for he knew not what. The occasional motion caught his eye, but his focus remained on the clear water of the pool.

Time passed, his mind blank and quiet, the eyes still watching from all around. He did not take notice at first when a different presence entered the cavern. The whispering quieted and the figures ceased to move in the corners of his vision.

"Have you no words to speak?" Vesth felt a pang in his chest as the sweet words reached his ears. He stood silently, all attention focused on the ripples of the pool. The presence waited a moment before speaking again.

"Are you so in awe of our home that you have been struck dumb? Or perhaps you know of what lurks and your fear paralyzes you." Vesth felt someone step up behind him and he heard a quiet whisper near his ear.

"Perhaps you came hoping to be released from your mortal frame." The sweet words became cloying and rancid and Vesth had to resist the urge to shudder. He moved slowly, reaching into the pouch at his side and lifting the letter he was given until it rested above his shoulder, never taking his eyes away from the water. There was a few moments pause and then the letter was slid away from his fingertips.

"A letter? How thoughtful of you. It has been long since I..." A quiet pause. "From Agamemnon?" Vesth heard the wax seal break and the letter unfold. The sound of grinding teeth set Vesth on edge and he was forced to refocus the pounding of his inner gates.

"So the Demon rears his ugly head once again." Vesth felt a chill run down his spine as the presence turned their attention back to him.

"You, swordsman, Can you speak?" Vesth let the question sink into his empty thoughts and nodded slowly.

"Then Speak. What does the one Pravin Solidus plan?" Vesth very carefully ordered his thoughts before speaking mechanically.

"I do not know what Master Solidus has planned. I know only that an army has been mustered. And they are to march against the High Priest Borsa. Others will march with us, but their path was not revealed to us." The room grew still and quiet. A figure in a flowing white dress stepped into view beside Vesth.

"Look upon me." Vesth carefully laid a hand against the smooth stone in his pouch and slowly turned to face the figure. The figure was tall, with flowing platinum hair that reached her waist. Her skin was soft and white and smooth as porcelain. Her face, however, was marred by an angry scowl and heavy dark lines beneath her clear blue eyes.

"What do you seek, swordsman? Why are you fighting?" Vesth could feel something pressing in on him, trying to dredge up his primal emotions. He very deliberately forced them down and spoke dispassionately.

"I seek only to protect the one I have followed. To be at her back as she fights to protect everything she holds dear." The figure eyed him up and down.

"Is that all?" Vesth's features hardened for a moment before returning to expressionless.

"To me, that is all that matters." The figure continued to inspect him. Then her form shimmered and changed. Twisting, pulling until Rielle stepped into the light.

"Vesth!" She cried. "I'm So glad you are alright. Its safe here. We can hide here until everything blows over." Vesth allowed a frown to curl his lips.

"Had you any idea of the strength of her conviction to help others, you would not even try to sway my path with her image." Rielle's features slowly became a scowl and she melted away, returning to the figure she was before.

"None will help, all will harm. Nothing is left but pain. Why should I allow men to tread in my domain to cause more pain?" Vesth fixed his eyes on the figure's.

"Better the pain brought by men, than the twisted corruption brought by demons." He took a step closer to the figure and lowered his voice. "Or would you prefer Master Solidus intervene as he did before?" Vesth kept his eyes locked with the figure, his power pounding in his ears, blocking out all else.

Anger, Pain, and a strangely defeated look crossed the figure's face. She breathed deeply and a shuddering sigh escaped her lips.

"Will you promise me one thing? Will you save this place? My charges have suffered so much already, I would have them see a glimmer of hope." Vesth stood quietly for several moments before closing his gates, focusing intently on the smooth stone.

"We will do everything we can to remove the threat of the demons forever. Even if our own lives reach their end as we do." The figure slowly turned and walked away, stepping into the pool and wading across to lounge next to the crystals.

"You are free to come and go, swordsman. My fairies will remain here during Master Solidus' campaign. I will put my faith, my hope, in you and the young cloak bearer." Vesth bowed deeply.

"Thank you. Should we survive, should we succeed, Rielle will do whatever she can to help you. Of that I am most certain." The figure nodded and rested her head against the crystals and closed her eyes.

"Then I will rest, and await your return." Vesth bowed once more then turned back the way he had come.

* * *

Vesth climbed up the side of a small, hastily constructed tower. The sounds of voices giving orders, and the clinking of armor echoed off of the steep cliffs around him. He pulled himself up onto the platform at the top of the tower and found himself standing next to the High King.

"I see you have returned to us quickly." The King said, his sharp eyes scanning over the soldiers below. Vesth nodded, and then turned as he heard another voice behind him.

"I'm surprised you came back in one piece." Nysisset stood moodily in the corner opposite the High King, her arms folded tightly across her chest. Vesth nodded again.

"As tense as the situation was, it was not as bad as Master

Delgorin had me imagining it would be." Nysisset huffed and took a step forward, leaning in to speak quietly into his ear.

"You smell of Fairy kind, I doubt that Master Delgorin was exaggerating." Vesth shrugged.

"It is done, so it matters little. Our Campaign through the wastes can go unhindered now."

"That is good." The High King stated. He raised a blue flag with his right hand, and a section of the army below stepped forward and moved across the front of the army in the direction the flag indicated.

"I had wondered if crossing the wastes would become an obstacle. In the past, if one wished to visit Tyr' Anon you had to have a guide who could lead you on safe paths to the city, or risk being lost to the wastes."

"Is Tyr' Anon our Goal?" Vesth asked. The High King shook his head.

"I do not believe so. Master Solidus told me to march east, keeping the Southern Serpent's Tongue just visible on our horizon." As he spoke, the High King lifted a small yellow flag in his right hand, and another section of the army below followed the instruction. Vesth glanced back at Nysisset, but she only shrugged, as if to say she didn't know. Vesth turned back to the High King.

"I suppose that begs a more pressing question, how are we to enter the Wastes of Telatia? The Gate here was destroyed much the same as the Great Northern Gate was." The High King nodded.

"That will be the most difficult part I believe. But there is a plan already in motion. We will worry about that when the army has finished assembling." Vesth felt a tap on his shoulder and looked back at Nysisset, who motioned to the ground below them. Vesth looked down to see Segine waving at him. The High King also seemed to have noticed.

"Head down and speak with Segine, I know Lady Marina was giving him instructions. When you are done with what ever she requires of you, I would like you to go speak with Commander Marstad. He is my battlefield Commander here, he will give you assignments." The High King spared a glance over his shoulder at Vesth.

"I have need of good soldiers to help lead these men. Many have never seen real combat, and I will need your experience to help direct them." Vesth placed one fist over his heart.

"My sword is yours. I will do everything in my power to help make this campaign successful." The High King nodded with a smile and turned back to the army.

"Thank you, Captain. I will leave things in your capable hands." Vesth gave a shallow bow to the high king and spared a nod to Nysisset before climbing back down the tower and crossing the dusty ground to Segine. Segine reached out and clasped hands with Vesth as he drew near, though no smile showed on his face.

"Is all well Segine?" Vesth asked, immediately noticing the knight's soberness. Segine paused a moment and nodded.

"As well as it can be I believe. Though if I understand the plan, which I likely do not, things will not be so for long." Vesth frowned.

"I am afraid I agree. But there is likely not much else we can do about it." Vesth paused for a moment. "Though I feel something pressing me to move forward. Almost as if something wants me to draw my sword and fight." Segine nodded.

"Then you and I feel the same. And despite what she might say, I believe Nysisset feels it as well. I've noticed her sword arm is restless today. I think that is why she chooses to isolate herself atop the High King's tower. But enough speculation, Lady Marina wished to speak with you. She had something for you before we start Master Solidus' plan." Vesth gave a short nod.

"Then lead the way." Segine turned and walked past the rows of soldiers and back towards the main camp. Soldiers leapt out of the way of the knight's path and saluted stiffly as they passed.

"They do not seem very pleased to see us here." Vesth observed. Segined harrumphed.

"I believe they have already been told we are to be their commanding officers. They are none too pleased to be under the command of strangers they have never met." Vesth thought quietly on this until he heard the strike of metal on metal.

Looking ahead, he saw a makeshift blacksmith set up beneath a large pavilion. Lady Marina stood in the center of the area, wearing a heavy leather apron and the sleeves of her robe pulled up to her shoulders and tied behind her.

She raised a hammer and struck a long two handed sword several times before sliding it back into a hastily constructed furnace and pumping a set of bellows beside it.

"I'm glad to see you aren't a gibbering mess after meeting Tyrannia." She said aloud as they approached. She pulled the sword from the fire and swung back around to the anvil and struck the blade with her hammer in a single motion.

"She was always a bit of an intense personality, even among fairies." She said between hammer blows. "I think she takes after Lady Sidhe in that way." Marina lifted the sword and held it out at arms length, inspecting the edge of the blade with an expert eye.

With a nod she laid her hammer on the anvil and ran her empty hand down the blade, instantly cooling the metal. Vesth glanced around to see if anyone had noticed the action.

"No need to be so worried Vesth. I set a protective enchantment around my forge to ensure no one can see what I don't want them to." She tapped the blade in several places and listened carefully as the metal rang before nodding and reversing the blade, holding the handle out to Segine.

"I have repaired the damage you managed to do knight. The blade is sharp and I have re-tempered the blade to better resist the touch of chaos. Should serve you well in the presence of demons." Segine took hold of the blade and inspected it himself before giving it an experimental swing.

"You are truly a master smith Lady Marina, Thank you." Segine bowed and returned the sword to the empty scabbard at his side. Marina nodded with a huff.

"I should hope so. Been doing it long enough." She turned and rummaged around in a pile of scrap metal and half formed swords before unburying a large chest. She lifted it with relative ease and placed it on the ground in front of Vesth. She opened the chest with a loud creak and pulled out a fine chainmail shirt.

"Try this on." She said, tossing it to Vesth. Vesth held the mail in his hands for a moment before looking back at Marina.

"I do not generally like wearing heavy armors." Marina scoffed.

"Some soldier you are. Leather armor is going to be useless

where we are going. Besides, does it really feel that heavy to you?" Vesth shook his head.

"No, but the design of this mail is generally made to be worn under plate armor." Marina smirked.

"So you aren't as dim as you look. Just put it on, you can complain after I'm done fitting you with a chestplate." Vesth grumbled, deciding it better not to argue, and slipped the chainmail over his head.

"Too tight around the chest or under the arms?" Marina asked. Vesth shook his head, rotating his shoulder as a test.

"It fits well enough." Marina grunted and pulled a grey-ish white chestplate from the chest and walked over to face Vesth.

"Arms up." Vesth did as he was told, holding in another grumble. Marina lifted the chestplate over his head and let it rest on his shoulders, connecting clasps under his arms and at his waist. To Vesth's surprise the armor was very light, no heavier than the mail he was wearing beneath it.

"What is this armor?" Marina adjusted a few more things and then stepped back, nodding with a satisfied grunt.

"It is the armor that was worn in Ancient Alenon. Designed to be lightweight enough to allow mages of old to wear without hindrance, but strong enough to take any blow. Be it from weapons of war, or magic, or the foul touch of demons. I haven't crafted it since the age of war, but it seems I still remember how to do it." Another nod and Marina turned back to the chest and pulled out shoulder guards, gauntlets, legplates, and boots.

"I assume you will have no trouble wearing these? Big tough soldier that you are." Vesth frowned, but sighed and shook his head.

"They should be no trouble. No heavier than leather soaked in sea water at least."

"And hopefully more comfortable." Marina said, dumping the armor into Vesth's arms.

"I have some for you and the Darkling as well Knight." She said. "You can change into them at your leisure. I assume you won't be opposed to wearing plate armor." She glanced at Segine, who quickly shook his head.

"I am not, though I would not dare speak on behalf of Nysisset." Marina shrugged.

"She will get over it, I'm certain." Marina turned and walked towards the other end of the forge again. But as she did she slowed and then came to a stop. Several moments of silence passed by before she glanced over her shoulder back at the two men behind her.

"Are you ready?" Segine shared a confused glance with Vesth, but said nothing. Vesth looked back at Marina and froze. Her eyes were vibrant and her gaze sharp, but she seemed uneasy, almost pained.

"We walk into a place long lost. To face an enemy of which we know little. With only an untested army, against a potentially numberless host." Vesth's eyes were locked with Marina's and he could not look away.

"Can you lead men, who fear magic above anything else, and command them to walk side by side with we ancients?" Vesth felt his fist tighten around the hilt of his sword.

"If they cannot, I will." The voice of the High King answered quietly from behind them. Marina shifted her gaze, and Vesth was able to tear his eyes away and turn to face the High

King. The King's face was an expressionless stone, a picture of strength Vesth had never seen before.

"Master Delgorin has returned. It is time we move." Marina raised one eyebrow in surprise.

"Already? I thought it would be a day or more before the army was ready." The High King shook his head.

"They are not ready. But something shifts in the wind, and the earth calls from beneath our feet. Something warns me that we have not the time to wait, and Master Delgorin feels it as well." Marina stared blankly for several moments before her eyes narrowed and a frown curled her lip.

"Fafnir speaks from the deep earth. If She has awakened now..." She trailed off, her eyes glazing slightly for a moment. She shook her head.

"Then we must move immediately." Marina resumed her march across the pavilion, knocking aside a pile of scrap metal and pulling another chest from underneath.

"Get your armor on Knight, and find the Darkling. Give her no room for argument." Segine bowed quickly and rushed to find Nysisset. Vesth watched the High King carefully for several moments.

"What is our next move, your Highness?" The High King took a long, slow breath.

"We show the people that magic still has it's place in our world."

9

Chapter Nine

Vesth stood at the head of the army next to a large man with simple brown hair. He could see Segine shifting uncomfortably on the other side of the man, and he could hear Nysisset sharply chiding him.

"Commander Marstad, Do you know what the High King had in mind?" The large man beside him shook his head.

"He only told me that there was a chance there could be rioting within the ranks and to be prepared to take action if necessary." Vesth felt his sword hand clench.

"I don't like the sound of that." The Commander nodded.

"I agree, I've spread many of my most trusted and disciplined officers among the army. But I cannot guarantee that will be enough. The High King already maintains strict discipline over his men, if even he thinks they could become unruly, then his plan must be... troubling, to say the least." Vesth scowled, and loosened his sword in its scabbard. Morien stood before the rubble of the South-western Gate speaking to messengers quietly as they ran back and forth, relaying orders.

Vesth could see Delgorin standing slightly behind the High King, hood back, head raised proudly. He made an imposing figure, Vesth realized, when he wasn't acting the weak old merchant part.

One final messanger spoke to the High King, who nodded once and sent him away.

"Stay sharp." Commander Marstad muttered. Vesth responded with a curt nod and watched carefully as the High king approached the army.

"Armies of Galbrea." The High King's voice carried out over the crowded men and reverberated off the steep mountainside. Vesth heard the small amount of chatter in the ranks behind him quiet as everyone turned their attention to the High King.

"Today we gather to march to war. Not as people of Hortaal, or Laytrow, or Gentry, But as one united people. Our enemy does not care about your heritage. Your noble bloodlines. Your proud History." The High King paused for a moment.

"Our enemy only cares about one thing, The end of our lives, the end of our kingdoms, the end of the very world we live upon. He means to remove us entirely from his vision of perfection, and he will use anything and everything he can to achieve that goal." Vesth heard murmurs from the men behind him and immediate orders from officers for silence. The High King continued.

"This means we will be facing against vile enemies of horrific strength and power. Many of you have already encountered the Nibilus, the creatures of darkness that now plague our countrysides. They will likely make up the bulk of our enemies forces, but there will also be far stronger and more dangerous enemies." The High King paused a moment to allow any chatter from the army to die out before continuing.

"I thought long and hard about this campaign wishing to protect our world, and the people of all kingdoms who live in it, from suffering. I myself spent many nights seeking guidance in the temples scattered throughout Galbrea. And finally I received an answer from The Six." Murmurs, now of awe and surprise, rippled over the army. The High King shook his head.

"Though I fear many of you will reject their counsel out of hand. To fight the powers of darkness that our enemy calls upon, we ourselves must call upon the powers of light. Powers gifted to a select few by the great Deity of Light herself in the form of magic." The murmurs grew louder and Vesth heard several angry outbursts. The High King stood quietly for a moment as his officers tried to quiet the army before an angry expression grew on his face.

"This power is of The Six, It cannot, and will not corrupt as many powers in the past have done." The High King roared over the noise of the army and all fell silent. Vesth felt a shiver of fear run down his spine at this angry outburst and his left hand clenched onto his sword scabbard. The High King continued to yell over the army, though not as loudly as before.

"The Six would not lead us astray. They would not fail in guiding us down the path that would save the world they so painstakingly created for us." The High King paused a moment to breathe and regain control of his emotions.

"This fight is far too important for us to allow ourselves to be blinded by old prejudices. And any who still will not fight wholeheartedly for our world and face our enemy can step forward now…" The High King reached down to his side and drew his curved sword.

"And face my blade instead." Vesth felt several of the men behind him take a step back in surprise and a much more subdued murmur rippled through the army. Several moments went by and things grew quiet and Vesth had almost begun to relax when he heard someone push through the front line.

"My platoon will not march into a battle, only to be destroyed by the violent nature of magic." The High King beckoned with his empty hand.

"Step forward Soldier. Tell me what you think will happen to us if we allow a select number of magic users, sent to us by The Six, to fight at our side." The man walked forward, a dozen men following behind him.

"Magic is a vile and dangerous practice. It causes death and destruction wherever it is found. It can even maim those who merely come into contact with it. That is why the purge was held, to rid our world of the corrupting power." The High King nodded.

"And how do you know this?" The man puffed out his chest.

"We were all taught this from a young age. Our elders taught us, and their elders taught them." The High King nodded again.

"And how did they know?" The man blinked.

"They, were taught the same as us." The High King nodded.

"And how would they know what magic does or does not do? The Purge was over 800 years ago. Caused by those who feared magic would end the newly established Age of Peace. How would anyone have a clear enough memory of so long ago to know exactly what happened? There are many books in libraries all across Galbrea from long before the purge. Why do none of those books mention this terrible 'corruption' caused by magic? If magic destroys all, how did our world survive all the thousands of years before the purge?" The man stood dumbfounded at the High King's constant barrage of questions before finally sputtering out an answer.

"The fact that there was a purge proves that it was necessary." The High King shook his head.

"No, the purge only proves that the people of that time allowed fear to rule them. We cannot make their same mistakes." Vesth heard the men behind him shifting uneasily. The man before the High King was silent for a moment, but Vesth could see he was shaking.

"My platoon will not march beside magic users." He finally spoke, and the tremor in his voice told Vesth he was afraid. The High King sighed and then shifted into a low stance, his sword pointed at the ground before him. His empty hand made a wide circle around his side before coming to rest lightly on the pommel.

"Then all who oppose my orders step forward and face me. If you will not fight by my side, then here and now, you fall by my sword." The men that had stepped forward all drew their swords. With a grunt, Vesth reached for his own.

"Stay your hand Captain." Commander Marstad ordered. Vesth blinked in surprise, but let his hand fall back to his side. The men before them spread out and encircled the High King, their swords held in both hands. Vesth looked nervously up at Commander Marstad, who simply shook his head.

The entire area was still. The tension in the air was enough to set fire to it, and even the wind had ceased to blow. Vesth could see a coiled dragon at the base of the longsword held by the man who had spoken against the plan to use magic, and he could not keep his shoulders from growing tense.

The man looked nervously around at the others and then raised his sword above his head and shouted before running at the High King. The other men did the same and rushed forwards, swords held high.

As they closed in, The High King twisted, grasping the pommel of his sword in his empty hand, and knocked every assailant off balance by striking the ends of their swords. Two of the men had their swords wrenched from their grasps by the force of the blow, and before they could even turn to retrieve them, they were cut down by a flurry of overarching blows.

Vesth watched, completely stunned, as the High King twisted and turned, fighting with a speed and grace that he had never seen before. Each swing of the High King's sword deflected multiple blows, and transferred smoothly into the next swing, making it appear as if the High King fought his entire battle with a single, smooth, overarching attack.

Even though the men were trying to attack all at once, The High King kept them off balance with his constant barrage of blows, and one by one they fell. After mere moments only the first man who had spoken remained, gripping his sword so tightly his knuckles turned white. The High King walked slowly towards him sword held out to his side in one hand. The man was breathing heavily, and shaking so badly his sword was barely even pointing forward.

With one more shout the man lunged forward to strike. The High King stepped forward and met him, striking his sword from his hand before landing several strikes faster than the eye could follow, sending the man sprawling backwards into the dirt before landing unceremoniously on his side.

The High King swung his sword to remove any blood on the blade and then returned it to his scabbard with a spinning flourish. He looked out over the army, most of whom had their heads half bowed and their fists placed firmly over their hearts.

"The divine power of The Six that was used to make each and every one of us cannot be evil. And even if it could be used to harm, how would that death be any worse than the one these men faced?" The High King motioned behind him.

"If we are to have any hope of facing our great enemy, who has begun using dark and twisted arts, we must all band together and pray to The Six for success and accept their aid." The High King held his arms out before him.

"Is there any man here, who does not believe The Six can save us?" The army was silent.

"Who here then will stand and fight for The Six? For our homes? For our families? For our world?" The soldiers all looked back and forth, muttering nervously. Vesth flinched as Commander Marstad stepped forward.

"I will fight, High King." Vesth set his jaw, willing himself to act, and also stepped forward.

"I will fight, High King." Vesth saw Segine step up next to the Commander.

"I will fight, High King." Vesth nearly jerked in surprise as Nysisset's voice rang out over the army.

"I will fight, High King!" The army stirred and the mumur grew louder.

"I will fight." Vesth heard another call from somewhere within the army.

"I will fight." Another voice, and another, and another joined the chorus until the call was an overwhelming roar of thousands of voices. The High King held up his hands and the roar slowly died down.

"Then let us all prepare. First, though they wished to turn us against The Six, we will give these men a proper burial." The High King waved at the men on the ground.

"Then we will set forward, with the aid of those chosen by The Six, and march onward to face the enemy who has waged this war on us. We will show him that we will not lay quietly by while he seeks our destruction." The soldiers all slammed their fists against their chests and let out a shout that rang off the mountains and into the plains.

The High King placed his fist on his chest and returned their salute before motioning for Vesth and the others to join him. Vesth and Segine followed along behind Commander Marstad, Nysisset lagging a bit behind, watching the captains order their men to move. The High King sighed as they approached.

"I hope The Six will forgive me for embellishing a little." Vesth nodded.

"I have no doubt they will. I think they weigh the fall of Borsa a bit more than they do a few white lies." Nysisset scoffed.

"The purpose and result are what is important. Just look at all the things Master Solidus has done. If he is still allowed to run free, then you will be more than fine. Besides, I think Master Khornal would have been greatly entertained by your speech." The High King let out an unamused chuckle.

"I am glad to hear that, though I wish that I could have spoken more convincingly so I could have avoided the bloodshed." Vesth glanced back at men who were wrapping the dead in plain gray cloth.

"It is most unfortunate, to be sure." Vesth said, turning back to the High King. "But may I say, your swordsmanship is astounding. I have never seen a display of such skill." The High King nodded slowly.

"I am sorry to say it is one of my very few talents." Nysisset nodded.

"But even I believe your skill should be applauded. I'm sure you are like the Knight here, and don't like bloodshed." She said, while elbowing Segine in the ribs. "But that said, I have never seen a human other than Master Solidus wield a blade that could match yours."

"I hate to agree with Nysisset," Marina said, walking up to them, Delgorin in tow. "But watching you just now makes me think that it might be time for me to forge you a new Blade." The High King half bowed.

"Thank you Lady Marina, but I do not think I am so skilled as to deserve a Soaring Dragon." Marina smiled warmly.

"Well perhaps if everything turns out well after this campaign, we will have Solidus test you and decide himself. It is obvious you already meet the prerequisites. Fighting more than a dozen men without receiving a blow is no mean feat, especially against another Dragon Blade." The High King shook his head.

"I did only what I had to do, no more. I do not need praise for such a thing. Besides, for now we have other issues we must attend to." Marina nodded.

"Of course, that's why I brought the Coot with me." Delgorin glanced around then exposed his teeth in a flat grin. The High King nodded to Delgorin.

"Thank you for your assistance Master Delgorin." Delgorin laughed.

"Ha, no need to thank me yet lad. Wait until we get back before we start anything like that. I'm not even sure what you want me to do. Opening a gate through the wall here is simple enough, but you mentioned something else was going to be needed." The High King nodded again.

"Yes, I plan on sending Captain Vesth and Captain Segine ahead with a small number of Soldiers to scout out what the conditions of the battlefield will be. I know sending a large army through too close will put Borsa on alert. But if we only send maybe a few dozen soldiers, and keep them perhaps a half day's journey from our destination, we may be able to sneak close enough to get some much needed information." Delgorin scratched his beard in thought.

"Hmm. I might could slip a few people in at a time without making so much of a disturbance as to draw attention." Delgorin grinned widely. "You're a smart lad. Solidus was right in choosing you to take command here." The High King smiled.

"Thank you for your vote of confidence." The High King turned to Vesth.

"Are you ready? I have assigned you the men I felt were least likely to bolt at the first sign of magic." Vesth nodded.

"I am. We will do our best to surveil the battlefield and relay any information we can back to you before the army arrives." The High King patted Vesth on the shoulder.

"Just do what you can, if things start to look dangerous then pull back. If there is a safe place some distance away to make a base camp, that may also be a good option." Vesth placed his fist on his chest.

"I'm sure that between Segine and myself, we can get everything in order."

"You hear that?" Nyssiset said, poking at Segine. "Everything better be in good shape when I get there." Segine nodded quietly.

"That was the plan." The High King nodded once again.

"Good. We don't have much time to spare, so rendezvous with your men and meet Master Delgorin outside the camp. We will meet you there in four days time." Vesth and Segine saluted and turned to find their platoons. They watched them go then Marina spoke.

"Are you sure you will get along with the Telatian while Segine is gone?" Nysisset harrumphed.

"He is at least quiet, and doesn't spout nonsense when he does speak. I think he will likely only be one third as aggravating as the Knight." Delgorin chuckled.

"Perhaps it is the Telatian we should be worried about." Nysisset shot a poisonous glance at Delgorin.

"They are both skilled fighters, I am sure they will be more than up to their tasks." The High King said with a general wave. Nysisset sniffed.

"Of course I'm up to the task. The army of the Brotherhood will definitely be ready for the battle when the time comes. If they aren't I will personally use them as ammunition for the siege weapons. We'll get use out of them either way." The High King chuckled.

"I am sure that wont be necessary. That said, we should get

moving. I hope to have the army mobilized before nightfall so we can get some distance into the wastes before we make our first camp." Delgorin made a wide, extravagant bow.

"Then lead the way."

* * *

Segine crouched beside a small outcropping of rock that jutted out from the cliff face. In the distance he could see a large citadel, built into the cliffs and rising nearly to the tops of the mountains themselves. He felt Vesth shift next to him.

"It is an imposing structure." Segine nodded his agreement.

"I am not fond of the idea of besieging such a place. It is all open ground and no way to flank behind."

"And no cover from arrow fire, if the enemy employs archers." Vesth added. Segine shaded his eyes, trying to pick out details though the heat that hung in the air.

"Our only options seem to be assault from afar with catapults, or quick jabs with small cavalry units." Segine heard Vesth scratching the stubble on his chin.

"I'm not sure how well the horses will do in the sand. Even then, the heat would only allow for a few charges before they became exhausted. And if we wait until nightfall, we will be facing Nibilus, who seem to be able to mostly keep pace with horses, so quick retreat may not be an option." Segine grumbled.

"Is there a way to approach the citadel without leaving ourselves open to attack?" Vesth shifted his weight around, peering out from behind the rocks.

"A shield wall perhaps, but we still run into the Nibilus problem. And a shield wall won't really help if the enemy has their own siege weapons. Our best option would be to try and draw out the enemy and lead them far enough away from the citadel that we could fight on a more even battlefield." Segine nodded slowly.

"That may be best, but we still have a lack of cover out here." Vesth sighed.

"This battle is not at all in our favor." He crouched down and drew a small representation of the area in the sand with his finger. Segine turned in place and watched quietly. Vesth drew a circle to represent the citadel against the cliffs, and then a semi circle some distance away from it.

"If we assume this is the distance at which we are safe from enemy fire, what tactics are available to us?" Segine studied the map for a moment then made several dots around the edge of the semi circle. "What if we place our armies around this perimeter, and then draw the enemy in to attack." Segine drew an arrow pointing at the center with the army.

"And then the rest of the army can rush in to either side and flank them." He drew two more arrows from the outside edge curving inward. Vesth studied the scene for a moment.

"That would likely be our best course of action, but I doubt we can goad the enemy into such an obvious ambush if we cannot somehow hide the rest of the army. Without trees or some other cover to hide behind, we are completely exposed." Segine stared at the map for a long while before drawing more dots behind the ones he had already drawn.

"What if we disguise how many troops we have? Try to hide them behind the main army somehow and make the army our own cover?" Vesth stared at the lines in the sand, a memory dancing in the back of his mind.

"Make our own cover?" Segine nodded.

"I'm not sure how we can hide a large force within another one, but it is the only thing I can think of." Vesth continued to stare for several seconds before reaching out and scooping all the sand from the drawings into a pile. Segine grumbled in annoyance and looked at Vesth, waiting for some kind of explanation. He was surprised when he saw a slight smile tug at the corner of Vesth's mouth.

"Perhaps not so frivolous as I first thought." Segine looked at the sand and then back to Vesth.

"I'm not sure I understand." Vesth half chuckled.

"Sir Segine, do you remember a time not so long ago when we fought in the snow, atop a mountain, with two certain young women?" Segine tried thinking back for several moments before he remembered.

"Oh, You mean the snowball fight at Master Solidus's home with Miss Rielle and little Tiasia?" Vesth nearly laughed.

"I'm not sure she would have appreciated being called little." Segine shuddered.

"I could imagine her shoving snow down my tunic again. Though I'm still not sure why you brought it up." Vesth smiled now, dropping a few tiny pebbles behind the pile of sand he had made.

"Do you remember how they bested us?" Segine stared at the pile of sand for several seconds before understanding dawned on him.

"They made their own cover!" Vesth nodded.

"Sand may not pack like snow, but I think we could still manage to use it as cover if we are clever about it." Segine stood up and brushed the sand from his armor.

"Then lets go see if our men have recovered enough from

their first time traveling with magic to start digging." Vesth grunted as he stood.

"As I recall, you did not look so well after arriving either." Segine scowled.

"Hey, I may not be sick from being transported here by Master Delgorin, but that doesn't mean I have to like it." Vesth chuckled again, and slapped Segine on the back of his shoulder.

"Lets get to it then. We want to be as prepared as possible when The High King arrives with the army." Segine grumbled his agreement and they turned back, away from the citadel, staying close to the cliff side to remain undetected.

10

Chapter Ten

The High King stood over the map table as Vesth and Segine moved figures around and explained their plan. Commander Marstad stood next to the High King, listening quietly as his sharp eyes took in every detail. Nysisset stood opposite the High King next to Brother Aegis with a frown on her face, though she occasionally nodded as the plan was explained.

"Once we flank the enemy the battle should be short." Segine said. Vesth removed the figures that represented the enemy that was surrounded on the map.

"Hopefully, the enemy will have committed enough forces to this attack that we will weaken him enough to make laying siege to the citadel much more feasable." The High King nodded.

"It seems tactically sound. What do you think Keliter?"

The Telatian nodded from his vantage point in the far corner of the tent.

"I honestly would not have considered this possibility from an attacking force, so it is unlikely the High Priest will consider it either. Though it will still be difficult to pull off if we are not precise. The citadel walls are high and offer clear vision of the surrounding area." The High King nodded and then looked to Brother Aegis.

"What of your men? Are they prepared to engage in this kind of complex strategy?" Brother Aegis studied the map with his arms firmly crossed over his chest.

"I believe Segine and Nysisset have trained my soldiers in the types of maneuvers required to pull this off. So as long as each captain can direct their men to do their part at the correct time, I believe they should succeed with little trouble." Nysisset nodded her agreement.

"I doubt any of them are smart enough to manage it on their own, but we have at least trained them to follow orders without hesitation, so as long as the captains understand what to do, they should manage as well as they can be expected to." The High King nodded.

"Good, Then I want the majority of the army of the Brotherhood to begin preparing to move out with a contingent of Gentry archers to act as the draw. The rest of the Brotherhood will join other groups at their designated stations. We should..." The High King paused as a courier rushed into the command pavilion.

"Your Highness, Something is happening." Marina entered the pavilion behind the courier.

"It seems our presence here has been noticed." The High

King rushed from the pavilion, everyone else close behind, and they were met with the sight of dark gray clouds swirling outward from the highest point of the citadel. The High King spoke without looking away from the swirling mass.

"What is happening Lady Marina?" Marina took a deep breath through her nose.

"There is no moisture here, even though the sea lies just across the mountains. Borsa is most likely trying to blot out the sun to allow for his Nibilus to reach us while the sun still remains in the sky." The High King scowled.

"Brother Aegis, Move your men now. I want them in position within the hour. We no longer have the luxury of waiting until nightfall." The High King turned to look directly at the older gentleman to ensure he was understood. Once Brother Aegis nodded he turned to look at the courier.

"Gather all of the captains and send them directly to my pavilion immediately. They are under orders to drop whatever else they are doing." The courier quickly saluted and ran off.

"Vesth, be prepared to give the other Captains their orders. Make sure they understand exactly what they need to do." Vesth nodded once and made his way back into the pavilion.

"Nysisset and Segine, I need you each to take a small platoon and guard the eastern front of the camp, in case Borsa attacks before we are prepared to meet him." Segine saluted and Nysisset nodded before elbowing Segine and dragging him away.

"What do you need me to do your Highness?" Keliter asked, his hand resting on his long knife. The High King looked him up and down then looked him in the eye.

"How close can you get to the citadel without being noticed?" Keliter glanced in the direction of the citadel.

"Maybe within a few hundred feet." The High King nodded.

"Good, I need to know whats going on over there. We can still draw an attack to us, but it wont do us any good if we don't know what is waiting for us once we make a move on the citadel itself." Keliter half bowed.

"Consider it done your Highness." He pulled his sand colored hood up over his head and slipped quickly away.

"Marstad." The Commander nodded once.

"I'll begin mobilizing the troops while the captains are being briefed." The High King half smiled.

"Thank you, old friend. We need to move quickly." Commander Marstad saluted and headed out into the camp as the first captains started to arrive.

* * *

Segine motioned for his platoon to stay back as he and Nysisset eyed a figure before them in grayish black armor.

"I didn't expect to see anyone out here so soon." He muttered to Nysisset. She harrumphed and stepped forward.

"Who are you? And what are you planning to do here?" A hoarse laugh echoed from inside the figure's helmet.

"I came here to break the pitiful army you've assembled here."

"Ha." Nysisset laughed humorlessly. "Pitiful though it may be, if Borsa thinks that a single tainted human is enough to break it, then he is a bigger fool than even I thought he was." The figure hissed.

"The Master does not realize I have come. He thinks to wait for the sun to be blotted before attacking, but I have been granted more than enough power to destroy a mob of worthless humans. I will finish you off now and prove myself worthy of even greater power, and get my revenge while I'm at it." Segine saw Nysisset stick her nose importantly in the air, and risked reaching out and placing a hand on her shoulder. She did not pull away, but she gave him a piercing look and he removed his hand before taking a step forward.

"And what need would you have for revenge?" Segine asked the first thing that came to mind, hoping to buy himself time to think of a plan. The figure growled.

"I lost everything because of fools like you. I spent years, decades, earning honor and respect. And all of it was ripped away from me because that fool of a commander would not listen. And then, when I returned to my post, shamed by the failure caused by the foolishness of others, I was slandered by an outsider and my post and title were stripped from me." The figure drew his two handed sword and leveled it at Segine.

"I will take back the honor that was taken from me. I will be important and powerful again, and I will not allow anyone to stand in my way." Segine's eyes narrowed. He could see a rearing dragon at the base of the blade, and the remnants of a crest on the guard.

"You were a Knight?"

"I was not merely some knight!" The figure roared. "I earned my way, through combat, into the Knight King's council. I was given command of the Laytrow cavalry and would have earned glory in battle if that Stupid Commander appointed by the High King hadn't done everything he could to foil me at every turn. Trying to steal my honor for himself." Segine scowled.

"Are you... General Proteus?" The figure paused for a moment, then reached up with his empty hand and removed his helmet. Segine's scowl deepened and Nysisset sneered.

"Look at what you've done to yourself." The man before them had ashen gray skin, completely bloodshot eyes, with brownish yellow veins reaching up the sides of his neck and halfway up his face.

"I will at least do you the honor of letting you know who it was you faced before I kill you." Segine took a deep breath to gain control of himself, then turned to one side and spit on the ground.

"I do not need honor from the likes of you, who has discarded any semblance of knighthood." Rage showed clearly on the figure's face.

"Tell me your name, knight, that I may return to Laytrow after my victory here and describe to them how much you suffered." Nysisset drew breath to speak, but Segine silenced her with an icy glance. He drew he sword and turned it to display his family crest.

"I am Segine Memoria, Son of Ignatius Cyprus Memoria, Grandson of Marion Carsolia Memoria. And I will not allow you to dishonor The Knight King, his Council, Or Laytrow herself by allowing you to have your way here." The rage on the figure's face turned into an intense hatred.

"I thought myself finally out from under the thumb of the Memoria family. But every time I think I have rid myself of one of you, another takes his place." Segine felt the brand on his shoulder begin to burn.

"You will explain yourself." Segine forced each word out through gritted teeth. He saw Nysisset reach up and place a hand on the side of her neck, and then take a half a step back to allow Segine to take the lead. The figure sneered.

"I faced your grandfather in tournaments, year after year,

trying to earn my place on the council, and each year he defeated me and left me in the dirt. And when I finally beat him, rid myself of him, I discovered that my shame would continue. I was forced to take orders directly from your father, and now I have left that world behind, hoping to be free. But even here I find myself under the curse of Memoria once more!" Segine growled.

"So it was you who was responsible for my Grandfather's 'accident'." The figure puffed out his chest.

"He was a necessary sacrifice on my path to power. I was offered the chance to gain true strength, but lives had to be taken for me to earn my place." The figure dropped his helmet on the ground pulled at a chain around his neck. The chain pulled free of his armor to reveal a pulsating, fleshy orb held in a claw of blackened metal.

"Your Grandfather was the first I fed to this pendant. And each person whose blood I fed to it has allowed me to grow stronger." Segine's fists tightened around his sword handle and he made to step forward, but a hand grabbed onto his arm and held him back.

"Let go of me Nysisset." He growled. The grip tightened.

"In a moment." Segine glanced over his shoulder to see an incredibly dark expression on Nysisset's face.

"Do you know what it is you hold?" Nysisset asked. The figure's sneer returned.

"It grants me strength, what does it matter?" Nysisset frowned.

"What you hold is a parasite, designed to eat away at your humanity and turn you into an empty vessel, perfect for hosting demons." The figure scowled angrily.

"A demon will simply grant me even more power." Nysisset shook her head.

"No, you would weaken until nothing was left of you, and then they would seal a demon inside you to devour what is left and use your body as a puppet. But don't worry, we wont let that happen." The brand on the side of her neck ran up her cheek and around her eyes.

"We will show you what true power is." Nysisset finally let go of Segine's arm and stepped back again.

"Destroy him." She said. "Teach him the consequence of attacking the servants of Great Dracolich Khornal." She lowered her voice only for Segine to hear.

"And avenge your grandfather tenfold." Segine nodded and marched forward to face his opponent.

Proteus raised his sword in both hands and leveled it at Segine. Segine grasped his sword in both hands nearly dragging the tip of his sword against the ground behind him, now almost running at the former knight.

Proteus raised his sword above his head, stepping forward and striking at Segine's head. Segine planted his feet, sliding to a stop in front of Proteus and swinging his sword upward to meet the attack.

Proteus grunted in unwelcomed surprise as his attack was halted midstrike. He tried to press forward and push Segine back, but was once again surprised as Segine matched his strength. Segine growled and batted Proteus' sword aside, swinging in a wide arc to attack his opponent's unprotected side.

Proteus mirrored him and swung his sword in a wide arc to protect himself from the attack. The two swords deflected off one another, and Proteus swung his sword in two more wide arcs, trying to catch Segine off balance. Segine scowled, spinning his sword and deflecting both attacks.

"You cannot hope to defeat me using the arts created by the Memoria family." Proteus took a step back and leveled the point of his sword directly at Segine's eyes.

"Your family may have developed some of the greatest fighting arts in generations, but you are just a whelp. You have only earned a coiled dragon blade, you haven't the skill of your predecessors." Segine raised the point of his sword and aimed it at Proteus' eyes.

"I have learned on my journey that the dragon blades do not prove one's skill." Segine could feel Nysisset's eyes on his back as he took his sword once again in both hands.

"I have journeyed long and the trials I faced have tempered my mind and body." He slowly began to draw back his sword, careful to keep the point aimed at his opponent's eyes.

"And I have been granted strength. Strength I have agreed to carry," Proteus gripped his sword tightly as he saw Segine's expression harden.

"Strength I have agreed to wield, with the express purpose… of killing you." The brand on Segine's shoulder raced down his arm into his sword, wreathing it in black flames.

Segine rushed forward, thrusting his sword directly towards his enemy's head. Proteus sidestepped and deflected the point of the sword away from himself with a grunt of surprise, turning to strike at Segine's back as he passed. But Segine was ready for him and twisted as he passed, catching the edge of Proteus' sword and knocking it aside.

They exchanged several arcing blows before their blades

locked between them. Segine could see rage building on Proteus' face, and the yellowish veins were beginning to throb. Proteus leaned into his sword, trying to press himself closer to Segine.

"I will not fall to the likes of you, a mere child of the Memoria bloodline. I will break you into pieces and feed my power with your blood. I will prove once and for all that I am the greatest knight, that I deserved all the honor and praise that the Memoria family stole from me." Segine grunted in disgust before letting go of his sword with one hand, Landing a crashing blow to the side of his enemy's head.

Proteus fell back several paces from the force of the blow, shaking his head. Segine flexed his hand a few times to straighten his gauntlet then took his sword in both hands again.

"No one took your honor, you simply failed to earn it yourself. You failed to understand what is required of a knight, strength in combat is only a small fraction of our duties." Proteus growled, an almost inhuman sound grating in the back of his throat.

"Without the Memoria family I would have risen to the right hand of the Knight King. It was my birthright, and all of you stole that from me." Proteus rushed at Segine, faster than before, swinging his sword with all his strength. Segine deflected the attack, feeling it graze the plate armor on his right shoulder. Proteus spun around, his ashen gray skin flushing bright red in rage.

"HOW HAVE YOU NOT BEEN BROKEN!?" He roared at Segine. "The strongest armor should shatter before me, Even the great dragon blades should break beneath my strength."

Segine glanced at his shoulder and, noting not so much as a scratch, he turned to Proteus.

"This is no mere armor. It was forged in the Ancient Temple of Alenon with the purpose of protecting it's wearer from the power of the Chaos. And my Dragon Blade was reforged to do the same." Proteus was shaking, unable to speak beyond gurgles and sputters of fury. Segine felt his shoulder begin to burn, as if Khornal had placed his hand there once again. Segine raised his sword in both hands, the black flames slowly dying down and coating the edge in an obsidian black sheen.

"If it is armor and sword you wish to see broken, I will gladly cleave yours in two." Segine marched forward, slow and purposeful.

Proteus face darkened to an even deeper shade of red. He raised his sword above his head and rushed Segine again with a horrific shriek. Segine knocked the attack aside effortlessly as strength flooded his arms and he spun his sword to strike downward.

Proteus raised his sword to block the attack and felt an incomprehensible weight press down on him. Segine stared directly down at Proteus and, for a moment, saw fear in the former knight's eyes as the color in his own turned black. Then, with a harsh screech of metal, Segine's sword bit into Proteus'.

One final push split the rearing dragon in two, flinging the blade to the ground and slashing through the old knight's armor from shoulder to hip.

Proteus fell back gasping for air, as oily copper colored blood oozed from the wound in his chest onto the bare sand. Segine took a deep breath as the black brand left his sword and returned to it's place on his shoulder. He felt, more than heard, Nysisset step up to his side as he returned his sword to its scabbard.

"Well done." She whispered. Segine nodded and she stepped past him. She walked up to Proteus, him glaring at her as she drew her own straight sword. She reached down and slid the fleshy amulet from around his neck, careful to only let it touch the edge of her sword.

Proteus growled, coughing up blood, but otherwise unable to stop her. She raised the amulet on the tip of her sword to eye level.

"This is not a tool meant to be in this world, let alone in the hands of mortals." She looked down at Proteus coldly.

"Too bad you were too blinded by your own greed to recognize the foul touch of the unnatural. But at least you will never make such a foolish mistake again." She raised her open hand, her brand draining from her face and spreading down her arm to cover her hand in a dense black blade.

"Let it be cleansed from this world, by the grace of Great Dracolich Khornal." With a swift motion, she slashed the fleshy orb in half. Shadows exploded all around them, obscuring everything for several moments. Slowly the shadows cleared away and the sun peaked through the gathering clouds to land on the sand once again.

Segine stared down at the ground in shock. Proteus had dissolved into a pile of dust, leaving nothing more than his armor and a few fragments of bone behind.

"He was even more corrupted by the parasite than I had thought" Nysisset said quietly as she sheathed her sword.

"But do try to contain yourself, we still need you setting a good example for the men." Segine shook himself with a scowl and noticed a smile touch Nysisset's lips. He turned to look at the men he had led out to this point and found many of them standing, completely awestruck. But as he walked towards them, to his surprise, some of them straightened up and pressed their fists against their chests in salute.

Segine's steps faltered and he slowly came to a stop as more and more men shook themselves and stood to attention, saluting. He watched for a moment, not knowing what to do, and then felt Nysisset's hand on his back. He didn't dare look back, afraid he wasn't fully prepared for whatever look she might have on her face for him. So he took another deep breath, then stood at attention and returned the salute he had been given.

"Remember this. No matter what happens, no matter what demons may come for us, They can be beaten. The Six grant us their blessing, and nothing will stop us from protecting our world." The men shouted, their voices ringing out in unison. Segine nodded and lowered his arm.

"Now we cannot allow any further delay, we must take our positions to keep the rest of the camp safe until the main force is ready for battle." He turned away from the camp, and heard the men behind him move to follow. Nysisset fell in beside him and matched his pace.

"Impressive speech knight." She said. Segine could tell there was some amount of sarcasm in her voice.

"It was the only thing I could think of to say." He grumbled. Segine expected her to laugh at him, but was surprised when he felt her hand brush his.

"But you did inspire them. More than anything they needed to have hope they could fight and win." She paused for several seconds.

"I...wanted to let you know, the spirits trapped in the parasite, I was able to release them." Segine looked down at Nysisset and saw the soft expression he had learned to recognize as her letting her walls down to speak from her heart.

"I felt Lord Khornal whisk them away from here when I did. Your grandfather should be well received now." Segine tried to think of a way to respond that wouldn't immediately cause her to close up again.

"You have my gratitude. Knowing he can be at peace means I can focus more on fighting here." Segine was once again surprised as a genuine smile appeared on Nysisset's face.

"I think you were the perfect choice to carry on your grandfather's legacy." She looked up at him and her smile slowly turned back into her usual smirk.

"I think I'm actually rather excited to fight by your side." Segine chuckled nervously.

"I will strive to be worthy of your aid." Nysisset gave him a short laugh.

"You better. I don't need you slacking off in battle while I do all the work." Segine grinned, glad to have some of his tension lifted as they approached the place where their plan was to be put into motion.

11

Chapter Eleven

Vesth stood at the head of a small group of spear men, scanning the dark expanse of sand before him. The thick black clouds overhead rolled past them, in great waves, blotting out what should have been the mid afternoon sun.

They stood silently, waiting for any movement. After several minutes, Vesth heard the distant rattle of armor.

"Ready your spears." He told his men quietly, and they lifted their spears in both hands in response. After several more moments, dozens of soldiers began appearing out of the darkness. They rushed past Vesth and his men, many carrying shields and short spears, many others carrying bows with arrows already notched.

Vesth stood, unmoving and calm, as the soldiers split to either side of him forming a large triangle with the archers in the center. Several minutes passed as the soldiers took up their position. Finally Segine appeared, bringing up the rear and making his way to Vesth's side. With a nod from Vesth, Segine turned around and raised one arm in the air.

"Pine Formation." He called out. Several soldiers moved in front of him with tower shields, planting one down and two at at an angle beside the first to form the point of the triangle. Two more tower shields followed suit, and men with round shields raised their shields over the heads of the men holding the tower shields. Vesth's men stepped forward and reached their spears through the small gaps between shields.

Vesth chanced a glance backwards to ensure that a similar formation was being taken up along the edges of the triangle behind him. Segine waited for several more seconds, arm still raised, until he heard a rumble in the distance. Segine dropped his arm in a sharp motion.

"Fire!" The twang of bowstrings sounded and an almost invisible mass of arrows whistled past overhead through the darkness. A few seconds passed and Vesth heard growling, and yelps of pain. Vesth drew his sword and Segine followed suit.

"Brace!" Segine ordered and the men holding the tower shields placed their shoulders against their shields, and the men holding round shields placed a steadying hand on their backs.

They had only a few seconds more before a sea of nibilus rushed out of the darkness and crashed against the shield wall, splitting to either side and surrounding the small army, many impaling themselves on spears as they went.

The tide of nibilus continued to flow around them, Segine and Vesth, along with dozens of men with spears, did their best to prevent the nibilus from climbing up over the shield wall.

The nibilus snarled and yapped, throwing themselves at the shields and trying to claw their way in.

"Light!" Segine ordered, as he cleaved a nibilus that was trying to reach over the tower shields, between the round shields. Men at the center of the triangle began lighting torches tied to spears and handing them to the men closer to the walls.

The nibilus collectively screeched as the men thrust the flaming spears out between the shields. The fires only granted them a moment of reprieve before the nibilus were once again throwing themselves at the shield wall. They continued fending off wave after wave of nibilus until all that could be seen around them was the swarm of bodies reaching out into the darkness in all directions. Segine raised his arm again.

"Signal!" He waited a few seconds and then dropped his arm.

"Fire!" A burning arrow raced off into the sky from the center of the triangle. Several tense moments passed as they continued to struggle against the nibilus, now climbing over the steadily increasing pile of bodies outside the shield wall.

Then hundreds of bonfires blazed to life in all directions around them and thousands of voices roared as men with swords and torches rushed from hollows hidden behind dozens of man made sand dunes. Another collective shriek as the nibilus scattered, trying to escape the sudden burst of light from the fires.

"Contract!" Segine ordered, and the triangle slowly began to shrink as the men pressed towards the center. As the triangle shrank, shields were removed from the shield wall and raised overhead.

"Spears up!" Vesth ordered, sheathing his sword and taking a spare spear offered to him by one of his men. The triangle shrank until it became a rough oval, with shields held high overhead and spears sticking out from every available gap.

The nibilus continued to scramble, trying to claw their way into the new tortoise formation as the new army surrounded them, taking advantage of the confusion from the ambush to cut through them quickly.

Soldiers began cheering as the number of nibilus dwindled, but the cheers quickly died when the scrambling, frightened nibilus suddenly stropped running.

All the remaining nibilus turned away from the shield wall, no longer yapping and barking, silently lining up to face the new army.

Vesth swore as he watched from between the shields. Segine looked over at him with a questioning look, but could feel a great unease filling his chest.

"I've only ever experienced silent nibilus once. When a Basilisk was near." He tried to mutter, so only Segine could hear. Segine immediately tensed and began whispering orders to brace the shields.

As if to confirm Vesth's fear, a nightmarish howl sounded over the darkened sands and the nibilus charged, racing to a single point and breaking through the front line of the surrounding army. Orders were shouted to try and rally the men to break away from the attacking nibilus and form defensive squads. Segine grumbled as the nibilus charged away from them.

"Open formation and form a phalanx!" The men immediately lined up, each man with a shield on one arm and a spear in the other, and men with longer spears between them. But before they could begin marching to aid in the battle, a great black shape crashed into one end of the phalanx, scattering men in all directions. Vesth swore again.

"Get back!" He yelled, launching his spear with all his strength at the enormous black creature. The spear struck its chest but bounced off, never finding purchase. The creature turned to face him, shaking its black mane in annoyance, its muzzled face sneering and baring its teeth at him.

"I knew it." Vesth said, drawing his sword.

"Get them back Segine." Segine didn't even acknowledge Vesth, simply began making small motions with his arms to direct the rest of the men to get behind him slowly.

The Basilisk snarled, and took a step towards them. Vesth took a step forward, opened his first gate, and propelled himself at the Basilisk, swinging his sword at it's neck. To his surprise, the Basilisk twisted its neck at blinding speed and bit down on his sword before it made contact.

With a jerk, it tossed Vesth aside. Vesth twisted through the air and attempted to land on his feet, but he was forced to immediately roll off to one side as the Basilisk tried to pounce on him. Vesth rolled to his feet and opened his second gate in time to brace himself behind his sword as the Basilisk snapped at him again.

Vesth skidded along the sand, sword pushing against the Basilisk's teeth, trying to stay upright. Vesth clenched his teeth, planted his feet, and forced open his third and forth gates. The Basilisk slowly ground to a halt, raking its claws in the sand, trying to gain traction.

Vesth growled and, stepping to one side, twisted his sword to strike the side of the Basilisk's face with full force. The Basilisk was knocked over and thrown on its side from the force of the blow. It scrambled to get back on its feet and turn to face Vesth again, an obvious and intense hatred burning in its eyes.

Vesth frowned, noticing not so much as a scratch on the Basilisk's face. The Basilisk took a step forward, more slowly and cautiously than before. Vesth could feel pain racing through his entire body, and knew he couldn't keep his gates open for much longer. He thought back to his last encounter with a Basilisk and decided he only had one chance. He felt the 'key' in the pouch at his waist grow hot and vibrate as he forced himself to open his fifth gate for the first time.

The pain he felt blinded him as it became a searing, torturous agony, and he felt a pressure from within him that he was sure could split him apart if he did not maintain control. But as his vision began to clear again, he could see the world moving around him in slow motion. The men and nibilus fighting not far away seemed to almost be standing still, and he could see each muscle engaging slowly as the Basilisk prepared to leap at him.

Slowly, painfully, Vesth slid his hands as far apart as he could on his sword and gripped it tightly, aiming the tip behind him over his left shoulder. Then he leaned forward and took a step. The force of the step caused the sand beneath him to explode outward behind him and he felt the air press against him as he flew forward.

Vesth could tell by the Basilisk's eyes, that it hadn't yet perceived his movement. He took another step, throwing another explosion of sand, and leapt forward. He twisted once to add momentum to his swing and aimed for the Basilisk's head. He planted his foot on the ground as his sword made contact, and felt something in his leg tear as he did.

Gritting his teeth, he continued to push with all his strength and slashed forward, splitting the Basilisk from head to tail. He skidded to a stop on his uninjured leg, his gates closing on their own as his strength drained away. He fell forward, landing face first in the sand, unable to move.

He heard the Basilisk collapse, and a horrendous shriek as the control it had over the nibilus disappeared in an instant. Then he felt a hand on his shoulder, pulling him over onto his back. Segine quickly checked for injuries.

"Are you alright Vesth?" Vesth would have chuckled if he had the energy.

"I used too much strength." Segine laughed once.

"Well it worked, whatever you did. The moment the beast went down, the nibilus started flailing around like confused dogs. Some are even attacking their comrades." Another shriek sounded behind Segine, but it was cut short and the corpse of a nibilus slid to a stop beside him.

"And some of them are still attacking everything else." Nysisset said snappishly, joining them with blood dripping from her dragon blade.

"So I suggest you pay attention and draw your sword until they are dealt with." Segine cleared his throat sheepishly, standing up.

"I'll make sure some men are here to protect you until we can get you off the battlefield." Segine turned and rushed back to his men. Nysisset looked down at Vesth for several seconds and he thought that, for just a moment, he saw a concerned expression on her face.

"Don't die on us before we are through here." She said, turning away.

"I'll try not to." Vesth managed to rasp, but even then he could feel himself blacking out, his vision quickly dimming.

"I will hold you to that." Were the last words he heard before he drifted into silent nothingness.

* * *

High King Morien stood overlooking the aftermath of the battle, taking stock of damage and listening as couriers brought him reports from the various captains. Delgorin stood beside him, a somber expression on his face.

"Things seem to have gone as well as we could have hoped them to." The High King stated after another courier gave his report.

"Minimal loses on our side." Delgorin nodded.

"Likely thanks, in no small part to Captain Vesth's actions." The High King nodded.

"I am of course grateful for what he did, though I do hope it has not caused him permanent harm." Delgorin nodded.

"Indeed, he did something very few people can do, and I doubt he has used such strength before now. There is no telling how it will effect him. I am glad he acted as quickly as he did though, as it removed the need for myself or Marina to step in. I feel it best if we conserve our strength for any... unforeseen problems if we can." The High King nodded his agreement.

"I appreciate your aid here Master Delgorin, as well as Mistress Marina." He turned and Delgorin followed.

"Now we should see to moving forward with the next stage of the plan. We need to mobilize the army and move to take up a siege position in front of the citadel." They made their way to the command pavilion, stopping occasionally to receive reports from couriers or to relay orders to captains to take up positions with the soldiers under their command to be ready to move out.

Once they reached the pavilion The High King held the tent door aside for Master Delgorin. But as Delgorin made to enter he froze. The High King frowned and held the door further back and found a hooded figure kneeling beside Vesth's stretcher at the far end of the tent. He opened his mouth to speak, his hand reaching for his sword, but Delgorin beat him to it.

"I did not expect you to be here so soon. Has something gone wrong?" The High King's frown deepened until the hooded figure's voice put him at ease.

"All is well Master Delgorin." Rielle said, drawing back the hood of her cloak.

"Things are moving forward quickly, and Steadfast Lycan Railast felt it best to forego any test and grant me his cloak without delay. Lady Quetzalcoatl also deemed it important that my journey be quick, and ensured the wind was at my back during my return journey." Rielle turned to face them.

"It is good to see you are well cousin." She said with a smile. The High King could not help but smile in return.

"And I am glad to see you are also well, since last I saw you you had wandered from my castle in the night to parts unknown." Rielle half bowed, but her smile broadened.

"I am sorry, it had not been my intention to leave in that manner. I simply pushed myself a bit too hard, and it took a toll. But I am well now, and no worse for wear." Rielle sighed and turned back to Vesth.

"Though it seems that not all have made it through

unscathed." Delgorin finally entered the pavilion and the High King followed.

"Indeed. Young Vesth was hurt during the battle. But he saved many lives by fighting off a Basilisk before it could cause any real harm." Rielle nodded slowly.

"I felt it coming, heard it on the wind. Though I never expected to also feel him rise to meet it. I wish I could have been here sooner to support you." The High King shook his head.

"We all have our parts to play, cousin, we are here to support you as well." Rielle smiled once again.

"Indeed. Could you send for some water?" The High King nodded and turned to leave again, but Delgorin stopped him.

"Use mine." The old man said, pulling a small flask from beneath his robes. She held out her hand and thanked him as he handed it to her. Then the High King watched in growing amazement as Rielle dumped the water on her hands and then on Vesth. Her hands began to glow, covered in a thin layer of water. She placed one hand gently on Vesth's forehead, and passed the other over his chest and stomach back and forth in waving motions.

After a few moments she paused and then placed her hand on one of his legs. Slowly the light faded away and the water disappeared, as if evaporating.

"I've not seen the Cloak of Perion in many, many years." Delgorin said solemnly. "It makes me realize just how far down this path we have come, and that there is so little road yet left to travel." Rielle stood, and walked towards the door.

"But walk it to its end we must, Master Delgorin. If we don't, then we only guarantee that the worst path will be the one most traveled." Master Delgorin half nodded as he stepped aside to let her leave. But Rielle only managed to take a single step before finding herself being blinded by silky black hair, with arms wrapped tightly around her.

"You should have told me you had returned." Nysisset complained. Rielle laughed quietly and returned the hug.

"I didn't intend to sneak in without telling you. But I knew Vesth was going to need my help so I came here first." Nysisset put her hands on Rielle's shoulders and held her out at arms length.

"A poor excuse, but I'll accept it." Rielle smiled.

"I am glad you are well. Is Segine also in good health?" Nysisset nodded with a pout.

"Barely. I had to rescue him several times, but he managed to remain unscathed." Rielle's smile turned into a grin.

"I see. It seems he was lucky to have you there." Nysisset nodded again, this time a smile creeping back onto her face.

"Yes very lucky indeed. I am only fortunate that the High King and the old man didn't need me to save them as well." The High King smiled.

"We are honored to have such a warrior at our side." Delgorin bowed extravagantly.

"We are not worthy of such greatness." He said, managing to contain most of his sarcasm. Nysisset harrumphed, but Rielle saw a passing moment of relief cross her face. Rielle smiled and placed her hands on Nysisset's and gently removed them from her shoulders.

"Before anything else, there is something I must tend to." Delgorin stood upright, a slightly concerned look on his face.

"It is the best course of action, Master Delgorin." Delgorin nodded slowly.

"Do you need myself or Marina to aid you?" Rielle shook her head.

"No. Thank you Master Delgorin, but you and Mistress Marina should reserve your strength for later. There are still things we may face that the army wont be able to handle, and they will need your power." Delgorin nodded.

"I was afraid of such. Very well, I am sure you have a plan." Rielle half smiled.

"Not so much a plan. More like since I gained each of the Cloaks, I've been feeling something drawing me to this place. And the first thing here that makes me feel on edge is the sky." Delgorin's concerned expression turned to one of shock.

"You... feel..." He sputtered for a moment. "Like a tightening feeling? Pulling everything in towards you and then into the sky?" Rielle nodded slowly. Delgorin let out a long slow breath, stroking his mustache and beard with one hand.

"Master Solidus told me not to instruct you, that you would know what to do. I assumed he had given you a plan to follow." He looked into Rielle's eyes.

"But that wasn't it at all." Nysisset stared at Delgorin for several seconds before understanding dawned on her, and her mouth opened in surprise. The High King frowned deeply as the solemn weight of the air pressed down on them.

"What has happened to my cousin?" He asked the Old Mage. Delgorin never took his eyes away from Rielle's.

"The Cloaks granted to her by Soaring Zephyr Sidhe, Great Titan Perion, Blazing Pheonix Pariah, and Steadfast Lycan Railast have awakened her unrealized power. She can sense the Balance now. She is like Master Solidus. She is a Balance Mage."

Rielle, expecting shock, was surprised to feel a sudden sense of clarity wash over her instead.

With just a moment of focus, she could feel the sky twisting and folding overhead without looking at it. She felt trails of energy, bent at odd angles, leading towards the mountains southwest of her. And, as her senses reached out further, she felt great tears and rifts forming, unraveling the fabric of the world, originating from and dense blackness in the citadel to the east.

"You see now, what Master Solidus has seen in you from the beginning." Tiasia spoke quietly. Then Rielle sensed the little girl was joined by another, older presence.

"You have finally realized what you were meant to be." The voice was that of an older woman, soft and kind, like a mother's. Another presence joined them.

"Your strength nears it's peak. Remembrance of your power rises in your heart and mind." The deep, powerful voice of the Patriarch resonated in Rielle's mind.

"We will stand by your side and grant you all our Strength. We will support you until the very end, until you have achieved all that you were meant to." Tiasia spoke again, this time with a conviction that filled Rielle with warmth. Rielle took a deep breath through her nose and smiled, a tear rolling down her cheek.

"We come to the end." Rielle said aloud. "Now is when we decide whether the world falls into nothingness," Rielle raised her arms above her head.

"Or rises from the ashes of this war to become stronger than ever before." Rielle closed her eyes and willed her inner power to beat. As she did, she felt immense power flood into her from all around her. The power roared in her ears as she directed it into her arms and chest, reaching out into the sky and finding each ripple and twisted current.

With deliberate purpose she twisted her hands outward, and pulled her hands all the way down to her sides. Instantly the sky was split open from east to west, as if from the swing of a great sword, as far as the eye could see. The clouds boiled and churned, as if flowing down the rapids of a great river.

Then, a great wind threw aside the clouds and blazing light poured from the sky onto the sand. Rielle raised her arms to her shoulders and reached outwards, as if pushing something aside, and the clouds were swept away over the horizon.

Rielle slowly placed her hands together in front of her chest and took a deep breath, slowly lowering her hands until they rested at her sides once again. As she opened her eyes she found Nysisset, Delgorin, and even her cousin Morien, bowing to her in respect. Rielle's eyes flooded with tears, and blurred her vision as she was overcome with emotion.

"Please don't. I don't deserve that." She felt arms reach around her and smelled Nysisset's hair once again.

"If anyone, anywhere deserves anything, it is you." She heard spoken in her ear. Another set of arms enveloped her, and Rielle heard her cousin speaking in the other.

"Nysisset is right. You have as much right as anyone to be respected and loved. You have great strength and purpose. I have always believed that. And I will always fight for you to have every opportunity to be happy with what you achieve." Rielle sniffled, tears running down her face. Then she squeaked in surprise as large arms wrapped around all three of them from behind her and lift them all off the ground. Segine's booming voice sounded above her head.

"You are one of the single most worthy allies I have ever fought beside, and I will always be honored to call you friend." Rielle smiled, and then heard Nysisset harrumph next to her ear.

"You better put me down you sentimental idiot." The High King laughed as Segine sputtered and quickly set them back down. Nysisset brushed herself off after taking a step back, and Rielle could see that her cheeks had turned slightly pink.

"Your lucky I'm in a good mood, or there would be problems." Nysisset said placing her hands on her hips. "But since you said something nice to Rielle, I'll forgive you this once." Segine bowed deeply, face bright red in embarrassment.

"My sincerest apologies. I was emotional for a moment and made a rash decision." Nysisset harrumphed again, but Rielle could see her trying to hide a smile. Rielle laughed, trying to wipe away her tears.

"It's ok Segine. Thank you for your kind words." Segine stood upright with a big grin on his face, and scratched at his chin nervously.

"It just kind of came out. I meant every word though." Rielle nodded and opened her mouth to speak again but stopped as she heard a noise from the Pavilion beside them. She turned, and her smile lit up her face as she saw Vesth leaning against the pole in the doorway.

"You always were too hard on yourself." Vesth told her. Rielle felt more tears in her eyes and rushed in to hug Vesth as well.

"I'm so glad you are ok." Vesth nodded, and only hesitated a moment before returning her hug.

"Only because you made it so. No matter what you think of yourself, we all rely on you. You do far more for us than you realize." Vesth looked past her and saw a courier jogging towards them.

"But we can wait until our work here is done before we need to worry about discussing it." Rielle sniffled again, but with a smile on her face as she let go of Vesth. The courier arrived, whispered a few things in the High King's ear and, after getting a response, trotted off again.

"It seems that Commander Marstad has everything in order. And moral is rising now that the sun is shining again. We are prepared to march whenever we are ready." Rielle could see Delgorin get a big grin on his face.

"I'm getting excited." The old man said, rolling his shoulders to loosen them. "I haven't been this excited for at least a few hundred years."

"That's because you live a boring life you old geezer." Nysisset retorted. Rielle laughed as Delgorin pouted and even heard Vesth chuckle beside her.

"Then I think it is time. We should do everything we can so we can all go back to our boring lives." Rielle said, straightening her back, and doing her best not to cry again.

"Then we march." The High King said. "And we fight to the bitter end to bring back our peaceful world."

12

～

Chapter Twelve

"They are demon hosts." Keliter muttered quietly from his place at the High King's side. Two figures in dark cloaks stood to either side of the citadel gate, waiting for the small group standing before the army to act.

"How do you think we should handle them?" The High King asked, but Keliter shook his head.

"I'm afraid I'm not sure. I don't know the extent of their power, though I am certain a simple assault from the army would likely fail." The High King nodded and turned his head to look at Rielle.

"What say you cousin?" Rielle frowned.

"I need to get inside the citadel as quickly as possible, so I would rather not waste time dealing with them myself if I can." The High King nodded again. Delgorin unclasped his cloak.

"Then I suppose it's our turn then." He said stepping to the front of the group and shrugging off his cloak. Rielle felt her eyebrows raise slightly. Beneath the cloak was a hefty, well muscled frame, clothed in a clean white tunic and breeches. Marina joined him, clad in full Alenon plate armor, a longsword strapped to her side.

"Let us handle them, and you go deal with Borsa, Young One." Rielle nodded.

"Thank you. I will await your move first, then make my way inside while they are distracted." The High King looked over his shoulder at Commander Marstad.

"Make sure the army stays back. We don't want any unnecessary casualties, and they will need to be ready in case Borsa sends a force out to face us, or if he receives reinforcements from elsewhere." Marstad saluted and then turned and marched towards the army to relay their orders.

"The rest of us should be at the ready for anything else that might happen." The High King said, adjusting his sword at his side. Once he had received a nod from everyone, he nodded to Delgorin and Marina. Delgorin grinned and cracked his knuckles.

"Well Sister, shall we remind these demons why they once feared Alenon so?" Marina nodded once.

"Yes, I think they are growing forgetful. After today they will remember that it is not only Master Solidus who is to be feared." Seemingly aware that a decision had been reached, the two hooded figures walked forward, away from the main citadel gate. Delgorin and Marina moved to meet them.

"So at last we meet." Spoke one of the figures in a deep, hollow voice.

"Had I known you were seeking a meeting so fervently, I would have sought you out myself." Delgorin answered.

"That would have made things far simpler." The second figure stated, in a coarse, rasping whisper. "Though the embarrassment and fear we will cause here with your defeat will be far more useful."

"And entertaining." Chimed in the first figure. Marina drew her sword.

"You sound awfully sure of yourselves for being nothing but hollowed out corpses."

Both figures removed their hoods to reveal smooth, eyeless, noseless faces with needle sharp teeth exposed in sinister grins. They untied their cloaks and allowed them to fall to the ground, exposing bony, emaciated bodies. Dark tendrils began to reach outward from them.

"We have merely tossed aside everything unnecessary." The figure with the rasping voice tilted his head as he spoke. A tendril of darkness shot forward at Marina, who raised her sword in one hand. The blade burst into purple flame and slashed easily through the tendril.

"Your definition of necessity and mine are quite different." Marina stated, extinguishing the purple flames on her sword with a flourish. They raised their arms above their heads, their tendrils spreading out around them.

"Your ideals will not matter once we are through." The figure with the hollow voice spoke as the tendrils began to form a large black weapon in his hands. Then the desert sand exploded around him and he was thrown to the ground. Delgorin stood above him, shaking dust from his fists.

"Don't you know it's not polite to try and force your

ideals on someone else?" The old man said. The other figure turned to face Delgorin, but stopped short as a blast of wind shot past him. He twisted, his black tendrils shooting out with blinding speed.

Rielle danced gracefully around them, and rushed towards the citadel gate. The second figure moved to give chase, but slid to a stop, bending backwards to avoid two blades aimed for his head then leaping into the air to avoid a flaming bolt of purple fire.

Vesth and Keliter slid in the sand as they landed, jumping back to place themselves between the two figures and the gate as Rielle slipped through it and into the citadel. The second figure scowled as Nysisset and Segine came around from either side to join Vesth and Keliter.

Black tendrils shot outward from the first figure and Delgorin disappeared and appeared next to Marina in an instant. The first figure stood, arching his back and shoulders, bones cracking and popping as they slid back into place.

"We will break you all into pieces and present you to the Great One as a gift." The hollow voice rang with something akin to annoyance.

"When we are through with you here, the girl will be the next to fall." The rasping voice ground like gravel as the figure spoke.

"All of your actions taken to protect her will come to nothing." The figure raised one arm, then hissed in pain as a blade cut into it and caused several cuts in his unprotected side.

The High King dashed through the sand, stepping around the figure in a whirlwind of strikes and slashes. Dark blood oozed from the sudden wounds and several black tendrils fell to the ground and dissolved into black mist.

The High King danced between the tendrils and avoided counter attacks until he reached Vesth and Keliter. He slid to a stop, sword held high in both hands, his eyes blazing an intense emerald green.

"You will find us not so willing to stand aside." The figure tilted his head as the High King spoke. Vesth stepped to the High King's side and raised his sword as well, and Keliter did the same with his long knife. The first figure held out his hands, black mist pouring from him and into his hands to form two curved blades. His wounds stopped bleeding and began to close.

"You think you can harm us?" He rasped. The High King slowly shook his head, keeping his gaze fixed on both figures.

"We don't need to. We are only here to slow you down and get in your way. It is those with the blood of Alenon who will end you." The first figure hefted a large black battle axe out of the sand where he had been struck.

"Alenon has lost it's strength. They are no more a threat to us than you." The hollow voice was tense with anger, but before he could continue speaking, a bolt of purple energy shot past him. He twisted to dodge a second bolt, but was then forced to raise his axe to protect himself from a heavy blow as Delgorin appeared before him.

The second figure reached out to strike the old man, but Marina reached him first. She batted away the blades with her longsword, and incinerated several reaching tendrils with purple flames that floated in a large semicircle around her.

"Humans may have lost much of their strength, But I assure

you Alenon has not." Marina twisted several times, striking with her sword and unleashing waves of fire with each strike, forcing the figure to retreat.

The other figure tried to push around Delgorin, but the old man simply reappeared in front him and struck him with a rapid flurry of blows, knocking him back.

"Not nice to ignore an old man you know." Delgorin said, bouncing lightly from one foot to the other.

"Back when I was a youngster that would have been a paddling for sure." The figure hissed, and launched himself at Delgorin, swinging his axe in a wide arch.

* * *

Rielle wandered, through cold passages of stone and black mortar. The air around her becoming more thick and tainted the further she traveled into the heart of the mountain.

"Strange. I have never seen this place before, and yet, I feel I know it." She said quietly to herself. She grasped at the velvety cloak draped around her shoulders.

Continuing through each passage, Rielle searched for something, but for what she was unsure. As she rounded a corner a twisted shape leapt at her, teeth bared and claws tearing for her throat.

Without thought, she drew her sword and struck the creature down in mid flight. Rielle looked down and realized it had been a nibilus. She wiped off the Patriarch's blade and returned him to his scabbard before continuing forward.

She continued searching through the somehow familiar halls and passages, pausing at each fork in the path to let her senses flow around her before choosing which way to go. After several minutes of wandering she found herself before a large set of iron doors. She could feel tainted darkness seeping from between them and knew she needed to go through them to reach her goal.

She took a deep breath and planted her feet firmly against the ground. The stone beneath her reacted to her silent command and cloaked her in a layer of armored plates as she reached out to grasp the iron doors.

The doors hissed and sizzled at her touch, screeching in protest as she forced them inward. The smell that washed over her was horrendous, making the hair on the back of her neck stand on end and her breath to catch in her throat.

Glowing green embers piled haphazardly around the room cast eerie shadows across great mounds of flesh, bones, and fur. Rielle flexed her hands and arms, allowing the stone plates to turn to dust and fall back to the ground.

"I know you are here." She spoke quietly, feeling as if the ripples of emotion in her heart suddenly grew still. All the darkness in the room seemed to twist and pull towards a central point across the room from Rielle, and she saw two blazing red eyes open to look at her.

"So you have come at last." The voice was low and raspy. Rielle nodded slowly, though her hand rested carefully on the Patriarch.

"So it was you whom I have seen, watching me through the eyes of the nibilus and basilisk." The eyes bobbed up and down, and Rielle could vaguely make out the motion of a great mass behind them.

"Since I was awakened, you have been the only being I have seen that intrigued me." The walls and floor echoed with the sound of the voice, filling the room with a pervasive hiss.

"Human kind has grown weak since the Age of Creation. Only you carry even a fragment of their former power." Rielle listened patiently as the voice spoke.

"I have not come here to seek the power of my ancestors. My purpose here is singular, and satisfying your curiosity is not my concern." The mass behind the eyes shifted again.

"Perhaps it should be your concern. The only path to the peak of the citadel tower lies beyond this place. Only through me will you ever reach the Great One." Rielle frowned.

"Are you sure you wish to test me?" She said, power resonating in her voice. "Despite what you may say, the millennia have not been kind to you. All those who were with you here in the beginning have gone, and only you remain. And I see your tether to this world dissolving as we speak." The eyes narrowed and Rielle heard a short, guttural sound which she interpreted as a laugh.

"My freedom is close at hand, but that does not mean my strength has waned." Rielle shook her head.

"You have been tied to this world for too long. You are a part of it now. Once your tether is gone, you will be torn between this world and the void. What shredded scraps of you return to the void will be naught but fragmented memories. Even now you seek to find a way to preserve yourself." Rielle waved her hand over the mounds of flesh and bone.

"Using the bodies of the Fel Wolves as vessels to carry you away. What others have seen and named 'Basilisk'." Silence filled the room for several moments before the voice spoke again.

"They were merely a test. Little more than an amusement until I found a suitable replacement." Rielle's frown deepened.

"Do you honestly believe you could take me for your own?

I don't believe you do. Instead you have tried to take all the living bodies provided to you. Because you knew that by the time I found my way here, I would be far beyond your reach." A deep, feral growl emanated from behind the eyes.

Rielle held her arms out to either side, as if she were going to take flight, and willed her inner power to beat. A great mantle of fire sprang up around her, cloaking her in brilliant red and golden flames. Immediately the room was lit as brightly as if by the noon day sun. The red eyes closed and a horrific, unnatural shriek rang out as it's form was revealed.

A mass of limbs and claws, patchy matted fur, and hundreds of lifeless eyes reared backwards, flailing helplessly in the sudden burst of light. Smoke rose from it as its fur began to burn and its many eyes began to glaze and turn white, and then black, as the fire spread. The shrieking continued and the body flailed, but the main head turned back to Rielle, the red eyes opening again, blazing with crazed fury.

"I will be returned! The Great One will gather my essence once this world lies broken at his feet! I will rise again and take my place of honor!" Rielle lifted her head defiantly.

"He will leave you by the wayside as he has done with all his other 'servants'. Nothing matters to him but destruction, pain, and death. You are nothing but a disposable piece in the games he plays. He cares nothing for your fate. But at least I will grant you an end. A courtesy he would surely withhold." With this said, Rielle raised her hands above her head and swept them downward.

Fire exploded out from her in a roaring tide, washing over everything in the room. One last shriek sounded through the room before being drowned out in the flames. Within seconds everything was reduced to ash and swept away. What little remained was quickly blasted into a fine layer of glass. Rielle drew her arms in to her chest, and the fire died away, leaving her standing in darkness.

A few moments passed, and then the room was lit with a soft golden glow as Rielle lifted an orb of light above her head. She quickly made her way to a stairwell opposite the iron doors and began the climb to the top of the citadel.

* * *

"Frankly, I am a bit disappointed that Solidus hasn't seen fit to come himself." Borsa's voice was silky with an almost unhinged growl hidden behind it that made Rielle's skin crawl.

"Frankly," Rielle replied. "We should both very much hope that Master Solidus does not feel the need to interfere directly." Borsa turned away from the edge of the tower wall. Rielle noted that most of the cracks and marks from the last time she had seen him had faded away, though his hair had been completely drained of color, leaving him looking far older.

"I would disagree with you young lady. Not having Solidus here tells me that I have not yet drawn near to my goal. It is a bit disheartening." Rielle studied the old priest's face as he spoke.

"Or perhaps you have, but Master Solidus believes that those who have come to oppose you have the strength to do what needs to be done without his help." A strange expression played across Borsa's face, not quite a smile, not quite a scowl.

"Do you think you have gained such strength in so little time?" Rielle breathed slowly and chose to look out across the desert.

"You know I have, Borsa. I know you feel the pull of the world as much as those who have journeyed with me. It is driving us forward, filling us with strength as our responsibility to protect the balance grows. I am sure that even you and the one you host have also found your abilities and progress to be greater than you had anticipated." Borsa frowned.

"You think the balance of the world would strengthen those who sought it's destruction? Perhaps you are yet still naive, hoping I can be dissuaded?" Rielle shook her head.

"It is you who is naive Borsa. The balance itself is not concerned with good and evil, destruction or healing. What matters is only balance and imbalance. My power has grown, for balance to remain yours must as well. This prediction we find ourselves a part of, the choices we would make, the power we would gain to face each other in the end, all of it has already been seen. All that yet remains is the conclusion." Rielle finally looked back at Borsa.

"Can you not feel the weight of the world pressing in on us? Spurring us to end the conflict?" Borsa stared blankly for a few moments then he made an unnatural jerk and his eyes turned an angry burning red.

"So you have awakened as a balance mage little one?" The raspy voice layered over Borsa's to form a grating dissonance. Rielle nodded slowly.

"As my strength has grown, so has my ability to sense the balance. You, Dorialith, should know that well enough. Not being a natural part of this world has likely made you sensitive to its intricate ebb and flow." Dorialith chuckled.

"I will admit, it has been an interesting experience, seeing first hand the work of The Six. Though, as powerful as they are, their world is not perfect. Do you not think that is quite shameful for those who would call themselves Deities? Do you not think such an imperfect work should be destroyed and its parts used to create something of greater quality?" Rielle shook her head.

"The world is imperfect, but it is not yet finished. To destroy a work before it has been shaped to perfection, is a folly of impatience. Besides," Rielle's eyes flashed with golden light.

"You do not seek a new perfect world. You seek destruction, not just of this world, but of something beyond." Dorialith scowled.

"And what would you know of what I seek?" Rielle locked eyes with the old priest, and the demon inside of him. Dorialith saw a deep well of power racing within her and, for the barest moment, an expression of concern crossed his face.

"Master Solidus once warned me that, because I had touched the void, fragments of my memories could be left behind there. Fragments that demons like you might try to use against me if they could. I have since come to terms with my past but, in doing so I also found fragments of the void within myself. I do not know what it is you seek, that knowledge is hidden from me. What I do know is that this world blocks you from attaining that which you, and many others, covet above all else. You will do anything in your power to end this world," Rielle lifted her arms slightly to either side and a dense aura of golden power surrounded her.

"And I will do anything in my power to stop you." Anger built in the old priest's face. He raised his arms above his head, red and black energy swirling around him.

"This world will end! I WILL SEE IT END!!!" All trace of Borsa's voice vanished as the demon's power overwhelmed him. Great black tendrils the size of trees erupted from him, shattering the stone structures around them and piercing the mountainside.

Rielle reached out and pushed aside the tide of darkness with a great blast of wind and fire, and throwing a great golden spear directly at Dorialith's heart. For what seemed like eternity, the world around them slowed, fragments of stone, fire, and shadow hanging in the air.

Then an explosion of extraordinarily bright light blinded them and scattered the power that had been gathered there. Several seconds went by before Rielle was able to see again but, as her vision returned, she felt a shock pierce through her.

Solidus floated before her, several inches off of the ground, with innumerable silver threads extending from his back and chest. Borsa was floating as well, twenty feet away, bound by great silvery chains that extended into impossibly black slits in the air.

Rielle could see Solidus making small motions with his hands, as if weaving or knitting some unseen cloth. Each motion caused many of the threads attached to him quiver and vibrate.

"I must thank you, Dorialith." Solidus' voice sounded far away, but still carried immense power and authority.

"Your actions have allowed me to fulfill my oaths." Borsa's body squirmed, and the translucent image of a great horned being flickered for a split second.

"No sense in struggling." Solidus said, continuing to make his weaving motions. "I have already bound you to the void. As my thanks, I will not destroy you utterly, but you will never again be able to enter this place." Solidus pressed his hands together, then pulled them apart, silver threads extending from one hand to the other.

"With your banishment, I finish my work. Be proud in knowing it was you who made it possible. Goodbye." Solidus looked back over his shoulder at Rielle and a sad smile touched his lips.

"I am sorry." With this said, Solidus rapidly extended his arms outwards and silver threads erupted from him, expanding through everything around him and washing everything out in silver light.

13

Chapter Thirteen

Rielle felt herself drifting quietly in nothingness. The soft velvety cloak around her shoulders cradled her in it's softness. She didn't know how long she had been drifting but, slowly, she began to become aware of a small voice. At first it was a tiny, distant sound, but it grew and grew until she could begin to make out words.

"...Ri...wake..." She felt something nudging her shoulder.

"...Rielle..." Her name stirred her memory and she felt something pull at her heart.

"Rielle, wake up!" Rielle felt as if she were suddenly pulled downward and jerked awake, sitting up suddenly. The world started spinning around her and she felt herself wobble.

"Easy there." Rielle heard Vesth beside her and felt a hand grab her shoulder to steady her.

"Lay back down, you'll make yourself sick." She heard

Nysisset tell her, and she felt a hand slide behind her head and then firmly push on her chest, forcing her to lay back down.

"What happened?" Rielle asked groggily, blinking in the blurry sunlight. Suddenly Rielle felt a heavy presence beside her. Someone touched her forehead, then a hand was placed on her abdomen. A cool feeling washed over her and her vision began to clear.

She was immediately met by the milk white eyes of Lady Quetzalcoatl, and the liquid blue eyes of a man she didn't know.

"That should help you feel a bit better, little one." The man's voice was calm and as deep as the sea.

"Lord Leviathan?" Rielle asked. The man blinked at her.

"It is a good sign that you were able to recognize me, even though you have never seen my human form." Lady Quetzalcoatl stood upright.

"Let us leave her for now Leviathan, let her friends balance her." Lord Leviathan nodded and stood, stepping away. Nysisset immediately took his place and leaned over Rielle.

"Are you feeling alright?" Rielle nodded carefully.

"I'm ok. Just a little thirsty." Rielle heard a bit of shuffling and heard a cork being pulled from a canteen.

"Here." Rielle heard Vesth's voice again, and saw him hold the canteen out to Nysisset. Nysisset grumbled.

"Well hold her head up then." She told him as she took the canteen from him. Rielle felt Vesth's hand under her head gently lifting her enough to drink. Nysisset tipped the canteen to her lips and allowed her to take a few swallows before taking the canteen away and Vesth laid Rielle back down.

"Better?" Nysisset asked. Rielle nodded.

"Yes, thank you. And thank you Vesth, for sparing your water for me."

"Of course." Vesth replied simply.

"So, what happened?" Rielle asked again. She saw several emotions cross Nysisset's face, but wasn't sure what any of them meant.

"I think that would be easiest if we let someone else explain." Nysisset said, before standing and taking a few steps back. After a moment a tall, slim man with jet black hair leaned over her.

"Good to see you again, young Rielle." Rielle's eyes opened wide.

"Lord Khornal!" The Deity chuckled.

"Easy there, no need to get so excited." Rielle blinked a few times.

"Are we back in the Mercury Mountains?" Khornal shook his head.

"No, I am happy to say we are sitting comfortably in the sand of eastern Telatia." Rielle could feel a multitude of emotions welling up inside her.

"Does that mean we succeeded? Did the prediction end with the world in balance?" Khornal smiled, though more reserved than before.

"Not quite, its a fair bit more complicated than that." The Deity stood for a moment, seemingly lost in thought, then held out his hand.

"Let's sit you up for now, shall we? I think it will help keep you from getting too disoriented." Rielle wasn't sure she was going to be able to sit up, but she reached out and took the Deity's offered hand. An immense amount of strength suddenly flooded into her and she found it a simple matter to stand up.

"A chair for the young lady, if you would." Khornal said. Rielle turned her head to see Vesth pulling a chair away from a small table. Vesth brought the chair and sat it down, twisting it a few times to allow it to sit evenly in the sand.

Rielle thanked him and then sat down. As Khornal let go of her hand, she felt her strength draining from her again. She wobbled a little, but Vesth quickly reached out and steadied her.

"Thank you." She muttered quietly. Vesth just responded with a slight smile and a nod. Khornal took a few steps then turned to face Rielle. He leaned back, as if to sit, and the sand itself rose up and created a throne that hardened into black stone as he sat on it.

"Where would you like me to start?" The Deity asked politely. Rielle thought for a moment before asking.

"What happened with master Solidus? I was at the top of the citadel facing Borsa, but then Master Solidus arrived, and everything went white, and now I'm here." Khornal scratched his chin for a moment.

"Well, put simply, Solidus forced the world into balance, and the sheer amount of power he used killed you, or very nearly so at any rate." Rielle felt like she had gotten punched in the stomach.

"It's not quite as bad as it sounds." Nysisset said, putting a hand on Rielle's. "Your body was still very much alive, but your soul got partially separated from it. I was able to call you back though." Rielle nodded slowly.

"Is that why he told me 'I am sorry' before he did it?"

Khornal leaned back in his throne and conjured a wine glass, which he took a sip from.

"I am sure he was sorry for that too, but I think the apology was for... something else." Rielle frowned as she slowly felt more of the fog in her brain starting to clear.

"If it wasn't for this, then what was it for?" Khornal silently inspected her for a few minutes before answering.

"In no uncertain terms, he used all of you." Rielle blinked in surprise.

"What do you mean used?" Vesth asked, and Rielle felt his hand tighten slightly on her shoulder. Khornal took another sip of his wine.

"He directed all of you during the series of choices that made up this particular prediction. But rather than direct you all down the safest, easiest path, he sent you each down the path that would be most volatile." Rielle could feel herself becoming confused again.

"Why would he do that? What was he trying to do? Wouldn't that put the world at risk?" Rielle could feel anxiety building as she asked each question. Nysisset squeezed her hand, and she shook herself to try and calm down.

"To answer why," Khornal said, after another sip of wine. "It was to put the world into a weakened state." Rielle could not fathom why Solidus would make that kind of decision, and she was unable to put her questions into words any longer.

"As for what he was trying to do, He was trying to balance the world."

"How does that make any sense?" Vesth asked, putting voice to the questions swimming in Rielle's head. Khornal twisted the stem of his wine glass slowly back and forth.

"It makes more sense if you understand Solidus himself." The Deity stared at his wine glass for a few seconds longer before it disappeared in a puff of black mist. He leaned forwards and rested his elbows on his knees, lacing his fingers together.

"Solidus was conceived, and born, in the Temple of Balance. His mother and father were balance mages, and sought to bring their child into the world as close to the balance as possible. This had the side effect of binding Solidus to the balance of the world itself.

Without going into more explanation than necessary, Solidus used that connection to forge more connections. He wanted to gain the power to maintain the balance for the sake of my sister, the Deity of Light. He swore an oath to her that he would always watch over the balance until the day the world was perfectly balanced and he could join her in the heaven realm as her eternal servant." Rielle forced herself to carefully gather and order all the information the Deity was giving her.

"If he swore an oath to protect the balance, why would he try to weaken the world?" She finally asked, and she could feel both Vesth and Nysisset beside her nod. Khornal sighed.

"Again, put simply, He grew impatient." Rielle felt another wave of confusion at such an unexpected answer.

"His plan was to gather every connection to the world he could, over his many years in isolation atop the Mercury Mountains. Once he felt he had enough of them, he would choose a prediction that was yet to come to pass, preferably a large one with far reaching consequences. He would lead those who were tied to those choices and direct them to make the choices necessary to cause the most upheaval.

Then, when the world was being pulled in all directions,

weakening the bonds between the elements, he would use his connections like puppet strings to pull back and force everything into balance. He has spent the last thousand years making those connections and putting his plan into action." Rielle could only sit in stunned silence.

"You knew about this?" Nysisset asked, almost meekly. Khornal half smiled but shook his head.

"I had some suspicions that he was up to something, but I never knew the full extent of what he was planning until he was almost completely finished putting his plan into action. Had I, or any of the others known exactly what he was going to do, I assure you we would have put a stop to it long ago. Though once things began, I did stand by to watch it unfold. I was ready to step in if necessary, but I was also curious to see if he could do it. Do the one thing we Six could not, as he had the one thing we did not. A connection to all elements and the balance that held them together." Rielle quietly tried to start ordering her thoughts again. After a few moments, Vesth spoke up.

"Why was Solidus able to balance the world, But not the six? He had connections to the elements, but The Six together have control over those elements." Khornal chuckled.

"At risk of sounding a bit full of myself, our problem is partly that we are too powerful." Vesth stuttered for a moment.

"I...I fail to see how that could be a problem." Khornal grinned.

"It's a bit like trying to carry a delicate object, like an egg for example. If you use too much strength to grip the egg, it will break. You must use much less strength than you are capable of wielding to carry it without damage. Now imagine the egg is so delicate, that even disturbing the air around it as you walk by is enough to cause it to crack. How then do you move the egg to where you need it?" Understanding finally dawned on Rielle.

"Solidus was weaker than The Six together, and so he was able to get closer to the balance and make smaller changes." Khornal leaned back in his throne and clapped.

"Well done young one. That is exactly right. He was also far more sensitive to minor changes than we Six, and was able to plan for those changes in ways we were not. Reckless as his plan was, he has done a great thing for us and this world." Rielle nodded slowly as she began to piece things together, then she felt an incredible weight press around her.

"Forgive me," Khornal said, his voice echoing in the air around them. "I need a moment to speak with you alone." Rielle managed to turn her head, and realized the world around her and come to a standstill.

Vesth and Nysisset sat unmoving, the few people Rielle could see moving in the distance were paused midstride, and small bits of sand hung in the air from a slight breeze that had also become still.

"What do you need of me?" Khornal stood and made his way to stand before her.

"There is still a task we would ask of you. If, of course, you are willing to accept it." Rielle nodded.

"If The Six have need of me, of course I will accept." Khornal smiled pleasantly.

"Excellent. Then brace yourself young one, there is someone who wishes to meet you." Rielle only had a moment before she was almost overwhelmed by light and a presence of purity she had felt only once before. Several more moments passed, and Rielle's vision began to clear, revealing a woman with platinum silver hair standing beside Khornal. Khornal made a motion with one hand, indicating the woman.

"This is my sister, Gleaming Seraph Arata." Shock and awe struck Rielle at the same time and she tried to bow, though she was only able to lower her head.

"There is no need for such reverence, little one." The voice that spoke to Rielle was a light, clear sound that felt almost like bells ringing in the air. Rielle felt a slim hand lift her chin, and came face to face with a pair of brilliant silver eyes. The woman smiled brightly, and Rielle felt herself smiling as well.

"There, a smile suits you more." The woman said happily. Rielle felt her cheeks burn slightly.

"Now now, sister, lets not distract her too much." Rielle heard Khornal speak, and when she looked at him she could see he was wearing a contented, happy smile.

"We were going to ask for her aid after all." The woman straightened her back with a nod.

"Of course Brother, forgive my fickleness." Khornal's smile broadened, and it seemed he wanted to say more, but he held his tongue.

"Firstly," The woman said looking at Rielle. "Let me thank you for everything you have done. You have acted admirably, especially faced with such dire tidings. I would also like to apologize, and ask for your forgiveness for my Servant's rash actions." The woman bowed slightly. Rielle shook her head.

"Oh no, please don't apologize, there is nothing to forgive. Master Solidus only wanted to do what he thought was best so he could return to your side. I cannot honestly say I would have acted any differently." The woman straightened again and another bright smile lit up her face.

"Thank you, you are such a kind soul." Rielle felt herself smiling again and tried to disguise it with a question.

"What is it you would ask of me?" Khornal pointed upward.

"Look up." He said simply. Rielle tilted her head back, and saw they were just outside the citadel. At the highest point she could see a large, silver orb, floating above the towers and spinning slowly.

"What is it?" She asked, trying to crane her neck to study it.

"The Seal, crafted by Solidus from the seven great seals we Six used to bind the world together." Perhaps due to the number of shocks she had received, Rielle was unsurprised to hear this, though she still looked back at the two Deities before her to ensure she had heard them correctly. The woman nodded.

"It is an impressive work to be sure, but there is a small problem." Rielle felt her eyebrows rising and Khornal chuckled.

"Don't worry, the seal wont break. It is merely not completely finished." Rielle tilted her head to one side.

"Not finished?" The woman nodded.

"Solidus was a bit...hasty, in its construction. Nothing vitally wrong of course, but there are gaps, and missing connections that should be addressed. But they are very small details. Ones we can sense are there, but are very difficult for us to see." Understanding slowly dawned on Rielle.

"You want me to find the missing pieces and fix them." Both Deities nodded.

"Indeed." The woman said. "With Solidus gone, you are the only balance mage left. More will be born in time, but you have been through so much, and understand the world in a way others never could. Of course, we would never demand such things from you. We would like you to do this for us. However, we only wish to give you a choice which you can make yourself, without feeling like you must accept.

"You have done enough for this world, and if you choose not to do this, all will be well. There is no balance that must be appeased now, the choice is yours alone." Rielle smiled, and almost felt herself laugh.

"I am happy to accept." She said. "As you said, I have done so much already. I see no reason I should not continue to do so. Especially now that the danger has passed." The woman placed her hands together and smiled excitedly.

"Thank you. I promise you, there will be great and wonderful things awaiting you because of this." Khornal stepped forward and placed a hand on his Sister's shoulder.

"Sister, we should not spend much longer here. Balanced as the world is, we do not want to disturb things too much before things have had a chance to settle." The woman looked lovingly over her shoulder at Khornal.

"Of course Brother, forgive me." Khornal smiled.

"You have long been away, I understand your excitement. But let us give them all time to rest before we set them back to work." She nodded and turned back to Rielle.

"Indeed, I should return for now. But there is one parting gift I would like to leave you." The woman carefully unclasped the Matriarch from Rielle's shoulders and pulled it slowly out from under her. Then she took the cloak and swirled it, allowing it to rest on the ground, as if over a cage or box. She placed one hand over the center, and Khornal placed his hand over hers.

"Rest well, Young one. And when you feel ready, you may

return here to continue your work." As the woman spoke, light radiated from her, and her voice began to trail away. Rielle averted her gaze as the light became too much, then felt Vesth's hand squeeze her shoulder.

"Are you alright, Rielle." Rielle blinked a few times and saw the rest of the world had started moving again. She turned back, but both Deities had disappeared, leaving only the Matriarch behind.

Rielle suddenly had a feeling, deep down in the pit of her stomach, and she slowly slid off the chair and landed on her knees before the cloak.

"Rielle?" Nysisset spoke with a slightly concerned tone in her voice, but Rielle ignored her. She slowly reached out and touched the cloak, and found that it was very warm. She tentatively grasped one edge of the cloak and lifted it. A mess of tousled black hair and a freckled face peaked out at her. Rielle gasped, and covered her mouth with her open hand.

"What's wrong?" Vesth asked, kneeling beside her, freezing once he saw what she had seen. The figure stirred and a tiny groan and a pair of brown eyes fluttered open. Tears started running down Rielle's face, and Nysisset finally reached over and took the cloak from her, throwing it aside. Tiasia groaned again and lifted a tiny hand to cover her eyes.

"Why is it so bright?" She asked. Before she could do anything else, she found herself lifted up in Rielle's arms, being tightly squeezed.

"Miss Rielle? What are you doing here?" Rielle cried into the little girl's hair for several moments, unable to speak. When the little girl finally managed to wriggle free of Rielle's grasp and look around she became obviously confused.

"Where is my room?" She looked around and saw Vesth and Nysisset.

"Mister Vesth and Miss Nysisset are here too?" She was surprised when Vesth smiled broadly and even more so when she saw a tear run down Nysisset's cheek.

"I'm really confused, What's going on here?" Rielle sniffled and finally was able to force out a few words.

"You're back. Lord Khornal and Lady Arata brought you back." She choked and couldn't get anything else out.

Understanding hit the little girl about the same time Nysisset did, lifting the little girl in her arms much the same as Rielle had.

"I will return quickly." Vesth stated, before standing and rushing off. Rielle hugged both Tiasia and Nysisset, and the three sat in the sand with tears in their eyes for several minutes until Vesth came back with Segine in tow. As soon as the big knight saw the little girl, his eyes lit up and he rushed over to them, stopping short with a concerned glance at Nysisset.

"Just hug us and get it over with you big idiot." Nysisset grumbled without looking, emotion catching in her throat.

Segine happily bear hugged all of them with a shout, lifting them all off the ground in his excitement. Vesth carefully made sure he was out of reach of the big man, a big grin on his face.

After several more minutes Vesth heard footsteps and glanced over his shoulder to see the High King approaching them.

"I think they are ready now." Vesth said, and watched in amusement as both Tiasia and Nysisset tried to wriggle free of Segine's hug. Segine set them all down, and turned away from Nysisset to hide his face.

"Master Delgorin is ready to take us back out of Telatia." The High King said with a smile, unsure of what was happening, but amused nonetheless. Rielle did her best to wipe her eyes dry and noticed Nysisset, with her back turned, trying to do the same.

"Thank you cousin. Your help here has been most welcome." The High King grinned.

"Even if we weren't trying to save the world, if you had asked me to march out here to fight Borsa, I would have gladly done it anyway. So think nothing of it. Once we return to Terramine, we will throw a celebration the likes of which has never been seen on Galbrea before." Segine's face lit up.

"I could definitely go for a banquet right about now." Vesth laughed.

"I am inclined to agree with you."

"Can I come?" Tiasia asked, rubbing her small stomach.

"Well we aren't about to leave you standing in the desert." Nysisset said, trying to sound annoyed.

"In fact, Segine will carry you all the way back on his shoulders." Segine spun around in surprise.

"I will?" The little girl looked up at Segine with her big brown eyes and Segine sputtered a few times.

"I mean, if she wants, I could carry her. Sand is notoriously difficult to march through after all." Tiasia giggled and let Segine lift her up onto his shoulders as he continued to explain why sand was hard for people and horses to travel through. They all started walking towards the camp, Nysisset telling Segine he was just a wimp as they walked, and Vesth falling in beside Rielle.

"Is it over now?" He asked quietly, only for her to hear. Rielle nodded slowly.

"I think it is. Master Solidus balanced the world, so all of the predictions that were made that come after today shouldn't matter anymore. Though I don't truly know if the world is safe from harm." Vesth nodded.

"Then we will be vigilant and ensure we are ready if anything does happen." Rielle looked up at Vesth.

"Are you sure? Our duty here is done. We are free to go about our lives as we see fit." Vesth was quiet for a while as they walked, then spoke again as they neared the remains of the camp.

"My duty is complete, but I will continue to stay at your side and support you." He looked down at Rielle and, after a moment, smiled.

"That is the life I see fit to live." Rielle smiled back, doing everything she could not to start crying again.

Epilogue

Vesth walked steadily up the stone steps of the tower, careful to ensure the crate he was carrying did not scrape against the narrow walls. Several minutes later found him in front of a door with light pouring out through a narrow gap in the frame.

Vesth gently pushed against the door with one shoulder stepped inside as it swung open. Rielle stood in the center of the room, surrounded by hundreds of candles, gently caressing the air around her as if pulling at strings.

Vesth moved silently across the room and placed the crate on a stack of other crates. He lifted the top of the crate and pulled out a small platter with a small selection of fruits and bread rolls. He pulled a small water skin as well and turned to place them on a small table.

"Thank you for carrying that all the way up here." Rielle said quietly, only half focused on the words she spoke, still staring into the air above her.

"You are welcome of course. The High King also insisted I bring you something to eat before you leave to speak with Her Highness Tyrannia." A smile pulled at the corner of Rielle's mouth, though her focus did not change.

"My cousin is too kind." Vesth sat quietly for several minutes, watching Rielle work before speaking quietly again, trying not to disturb her too much.

"Tiasia tried to pack herself into the crates to come see you." Rielle smiled brightly and slowly let her hands fall to her sides.

"I told her she had to study in Terramine and with Nysisset before she could come here." Rielle turned away from her work and, with a wave of her hand, extinguished a majority of the candles in the room. She made her way to the small table and sat across from Vesth, selecting a sliced fruit to nibble on.

"She just wants to see you, and help you in whatever small way she can." Vesth said, a smile threatening to appear on one side of his face, which he turned to hide.

"Would that I could see Master Solidus' Seal so that I might do the same." Rielle shook her head and quickly swallowed the fruit she was chewing.

"You do plenty for me Vesth. Without you helping coordinate everything for me I wouldn't have nearly the time to study the Seal as I do. You are a great help, I assure you." Vesth finally gave in and smiled.

"Speaking of coordination, Lord Leviathan left a letter and a message for you with the High King. After you speak with her Highness Tyrannia, Great Titan Perion wished to speak with you at his temple. Something on the subject of Blazing Pheonix Pariah having more contact with the Seal and the new balance mage than he, Though I am sure Lord Leviathan was more... cordial in his wording than what he was likely meant to convey." Rielle smiled.

"I have noticed that Lord Perion does tend to get a bit jealous when Lady Pariah is involved. I will be sure to visit him once my business with Lady Tyrannia is through. In fact I may need Lord Perion's help to reestablish some of the oases in Telatia. I am sure that will put him in a good mood." Vesth smiled broadly as Rielle talked, and after a few moments she took notice.

"What is it Vesth? You seem very happy today." Vesth sat back in his chair and looked down for a moment.

"It is good to see you in such high spirits." Rielle tipped her head to one side.

"Am I? I don't feel any different than normal." Vesth nodded and stood, placing a hand on hers.

"Compared to how you were months ago when first we returned here, you are so much lighter of heart than you were. I think you have settled well into your role." Vesth chuckled as Rielle blushed.

"Eat up Rielle, we both have work to do and neither of us is likely to have time to rest anytime soon." Vesth turned and made his way back towards the door.

"Tell my cousin and the others I send my regards. And let Tiasia know I will come back soon to visit." Rielle said, watching Vesth's back as he walked away. Vesth reached the door and looked back over his shoulder.

"Eat." He said, and then slipped through the door way, pulling the door shut behind him. Rielle pouted for a moment, but eventually she smiled and took a bread roll, chewing on one end before returning to her place across the room.

A wave of her hand caused the candles to blaze into life once more as she lifted her head to face the great silver Seal above her.

The End

www.ingramcontent.com/pod-product-compliance
Lightning Source LLC
Chambersburg PA
CBHW070343200726

48294CB00003B/771